MOONBC

Horror Anthology 2015

The Moon Books Project

Horror Anthology 2015

Copyright © 2015 Brandon Mullins

All rights reserved.

ISBN: 1518757731

ISBN-13: 978-1518757730

Chokepoint

Copyright © 2012 Jonathan Maberry Productions, LLC

You'll Never Be Lunch in This Town Again

Copyright © 2015 Dana Fredsti

Death Bringer Jones

Copyright © 2014 Thomas M. Malafarina

Kitties and Zombies, Oh My!

Copyright © 2015 Catt Dahman

Pleasure Island

Copyright © 2015 Wesley Thomas

Regret

Copyright © 2015 Dana M. Lyons

CONTENTS

Foreword

Chokepoint   Pg 1

by Jonathan Maberry

You'll Never Be Lunch in This Town Again   Pg 43

by Dana Fredsti

Death Bringer Jones   Pg 83

by Thomas M. Malafarina

Kitties and Zombies, Oh My!   Pg 93

by Catt Dahman

Pleasure Island   Pg 117

by Wesley Thomas

Regret   Pg 138

by Amanda M. Lyons

Foreword

Thomas M. Malafarina

If someone were to ask you what the greatest gift is a reader can give to an author; what do you think you'd say? Would you suggest the purchase of an author's book is the best thing a reader can do? After all it does help provide the author with a source of income. That sort of thinking would be considered very wise in today's literary market where thanks to the availability of internet resources virtually anyone can publish a book. My own publisher Lawrence Knorr of Sunbury Press says that in 2015 it's probably easier for someone to publish a book than it has ever been at any other time in history.

He also however, will be quick to point out in contrast it's one of the hardest times to sell a book. This is because the market is flooded with thousands of tomes by never previously published authors. So the purchase of an author's book is not something to be lightly discounted, especially if that particular purchase is made by several million people. (From my lips - to God's ears!)

Maybe you'd suggest that a favorable review is something very special someone can do to help their favorite author. The theory being that if someone has gone onto Amazon in search of a traditional book or kindle; and they see a number of favorable heart-felt reviews then that person might be more likely to purchase their own copy. Again, if a favorable review can help sell books and provide the author with an income then that could be considered a great gift as well.

What about free publicity? How about an interview in a major magazine or newspaper featuring the author on the cover? Or maybe a feature video interview for a major television show? I would think any of these would be a major boon in the career of an aspiring author, not to mention well-established authors. I'm sure the debate surrounding the perfect gift from reader to author could go on forever.

Now I'm going to tell you something that might surprise you. Something I feel is the greatest gift a reader can give to an author. It's their time. Whether the reader is a graduate of the Evelyn Wood Speed Reading course or a slow and methodical reader such as I am, whenever someone takes time out of their own busy schedule to read a book they are investing something they can never get back; a small portion of their lives. Think about that for a minute. Readers are actually sacrificing a portion of their lives, just so they can read what you've written. No small gift in my opinion and something which places a heavy burden of responsibility for authors to always produce the best product we possibly can.

So now we come to the part where I bring this book and the valuable time you are investing in reading it into the equation. When you first saw the cover of this book and read the title "Horror Anthology 2015" you might have thought, perhaps a little sarcastically, "Oh great, another anthology of horror stories. Wow! That's something really different."

But maybe this one is just a bit different. I realize there are dozens of horror anthologies published every month. I know, because I'm in about thirty of them every year. Sometimes they're comprised of authors with whom you may be familiar and more often than not with many you don't know. But that's the purpose of publishing these anthologies, these collections; to give you a chance to sample the works of many different authors all in one place. It also provides an opportunity for new up and coming authors to put their stories in front of the members of the public who might not normally see them.

You might buy the book for the authors you know and then as a side benefit you get introduced to new authors. It's a win-win situation for all involved. I often submit my own work to anthologies simply because it's a good way not only to get my name out there for recognition from new readers but to keep it out there so long-time readers know I'm still busy writing and haven't fallen into obscurity. And for the new authors out there, yes, sometimes I get rejected too; that's all part of the game.

Many authors work on their novels for several months or in some cases years before they are ready for publication. So what are readers who are starving for horror supposed to do while their favorite writers like working on their next novels? That's the niche that anthologies are very good at filling.

And every so often something special happens. On occasions, I'm personally invited to participate in an upcoming anthology. In other words, the editor has a specific group of authors that he wants to be part of his book. When I am invited I'm always honored not only for the consideration but for the opportunity. Often after securing his core group of desired authors, a publisher will then open the rest of the collection for general submissions.

When Brandon Mullins of Moon Books contacted me and asked me to be part of his anthology I was more than willing to submit a story. Then when I heard I would be sharing the pages with such authors as Johnathan Maberry, Catt Dahman, Dana Fredsti, Amanda Lyons and Wesley Thomas, I was even more eager to be part of this work. And as if that were not rewarding enough, I had the further honor of being asked to write this foreword for the book.

For someone such as me, who loves to write and who truly feels the act of writing is its own reward, this opportunity to speak briefly to you one-on-one before you begin your journey into the terrifying world of horror was very special. As such, I won't abuse that trust and will wrap this up quickly and offer a personal thanks to all of you for this most precious gift of your time with the hopes that you'll enjoy the stories enough to feel your investment was well worthwhile.

Thomas M. Malafarina, October 2015

Chokepoint

Jonathan Maberry

-1-

The lieutenant said to hold it.

So we're holding it.

Chokepoint Baker: five miles up a crooked road, fifty miles from the command post, a hundred miles from the war.

They dropped us here three days after what the radio has been calling First Night.

Couple days later, I heard a DJ out of Philly call it Last Night. But the news guys always do that hysterical shit. If it's going to snow, they start talking about blizzards; two guys shove each other outside a Wal-Mart, and it's rioting in the streets. Their amps are always dialed up to eleven.

Guess that sort of thing's infectious, because we got rousted and rolled before dawn's early light.

As we climbed down off the truck, Lieutenant Bell took me aside. We'd known each other for a while and he usually called me

Sally or Sal, but not that day. He was all Joe-Army. "Listen up, corporal," he told me. "The infection is contained to the west side of this river. There are two other bridges; closest is eight klicks downstream. We're spread pretty thin, so I can spare one fireteam per bridge. This one's yours."

The bridge was rusted steel that had once been painted blue, a lane of blacktop going in each direction. No tollbooth, no nothing. Pennsylvania on one side, New Jersey on the other.

"You think you can do that, Corporal?"

I grinned. "C'mon, Loot, a couple of Cub Scouts could hold that bridge with a slingshot and a wet fart."

I always cracked him up, drunk or sober, but now he just gave me the *look*. The officer look.

I straightened. "Yes, sir. We'll hold it."

"You are authorized to barricade this bridge. Make sure nothing gets across. Nothing and no one, do you understand?"

For what? Some dickheads rioting on the other side of the state? I wanted to laugh.

But there was something in his eyes. He lowered his voice so it was just heard by the two of us. Everyone else was handing empty sandbags and equipment boxes down from the truck. "This is serious shit, Sally. I need you to do this."

I gave a quick right-left look to make sure no one could hear us. "The fuck's going down, man? You got the bug-eyes going on. This is a bunch of civilians going ape-shit, right?"

Bell licked his lips. Real nervous, the way a scared dog does.

"You really don't know, do you?" he asked. "Haven't you been watching the news?"

"Yeah, I've seen the news."

"They aren't civilians," he said. "Not anymore."

"What does that—?"

A sergeant came hurrying over to tell us that everything was off-loaded. Bell stepped abruptly away from me and back into his officer role. "Are we clear on everything, Corporal Tucci?"

I played my part. "Yes, *sir*."

Bell and the sergeant climbed back into the truck and we watched its taillights through a faint smudge of dust. My guys—all three of them—stood with me. We turned and looked at the bridge.

It was rush hour on a Friday, but the road was empty. Both sides of the bridge.

"What the hell's going on?" asked Joe Bob—and, yeah, his actual name on his dog tags is Joe Bob Stanton. He's a redneck mouth-breather who joined the Reserves because nobody in the civilian world was stupid enough to let him play with guns. So the geniuses here decided he should be an automatic rifleman. When they handed him an M249 Squad Automatic Weapon, he almost came in his pants.

I shook my head.

"Join the Navy," said Talia, "See the world."

"That's the Navy," said Farris. "We're the National damn Guard."

"That's my point," she said.

"C'mon," I said, "let's get this shit done."

It took us four hours to fill enough sandbags to block the western approach to the bridge. Four hours. Didn't see a single car the whole time.

At first that was okay, made it easier to work.

Later, though, none of us liked how that felt.

-2-

I was the Team Leader for this gig. Corporal Salvatore Tucci. I'm in charge because everyone else on the team was even greener than me. Army Reserves, man. I'm in technical college working on a degree in fixing air conditioners, and I'm the most educated guy on the team. Cutting-edge, 21st century Army my ass.

A lot of the guys who enlist are dickheads like Joe Bob.

The other two? Farris is a slacker with no G.E.D. who mops up at a Taco Bell. They made him a rifleman. And our grenadier, Talia? Her arms and her thighs are a roadmap of healed-over needle scars, but she doesn't talk about it. I think she maybe got clean and signed up to help her stay clean.

That's Fireteam Delta. Four fuck-ups who didn't have the sense to stay out of uniform or enough useful skills to be put somewhere that mattered.

So here we are, holding Checkpoint Baker and waiting for orders.

We opened some M.R.E.s and ate bad spaghetti and some watery stuff that was supposed to be cream of broccoli soup.

"Dude," said Farris, "there's a Quizno's like three miles from here. I saw it on the way in."

"So?"

"One of us could go and get something…"

"Deserting a post in a time of crisis?" murmured Talia dryly. "I think they have a rule about that.

"It's not deserting," said Farris, but he didn't push it. I think he knew what we all thought. As soon as he was around the bend in the road he'd fire up a blunt, and that's all we'd need is to have the lieutenant roll up on Farris stoned and A.W.O.L. On my watch.

I gave him my version of the *look*.

He grinned like a kid who was caught reaching in the cookie jar.

"Hey," said Talia, "somebody's coming."

And shit if we didn't all look the wrong way first. We looked up the road, the way the truck went. Then we realized Talia was looking over the sandbags.

We turned.

There was someone on the road. Not in a car. On foot, walking along the side of the road, maybe four hundred yards away.

"Civvie," said Talia. "Looks like a kid."

I took out my binoculars. They're a cheap, low-intensity pair that I bought myself. Still better than the 'no pair' they issued me. The civvie kid was maybe seventeen, wearing a Philadelphia Eagles sweatshirt, jeans, and bare feet. He walked with his head down, stumbling a little. There were dark smears on his shirt, and I've been in enough bar fights to know what blood looks like when it dries on a football jersey. There was some blood on what I could see of his face and on both hands.

"Whoever he is," I said, "someone kicked his ass."

They took turns looking.

While Talia was looking, the guy raised his head, and she screamed. Like a horror movie scream; just a kind of yelp.

"Holy shit!"

"What?" Everyone asked it at the same time.

"His face…"

I took the binoculars back. The guy's head was down again. He was about a hundred yards away now, coming on but not in a hurry. If he was that jacked up then maybe he was really out of it.

Maybe he got drunk and picked the wrong fight and now his head was busted and he didn't know where he was.

"What's wrong with his face?" asked Farris.

When Talia didn't answer, I lowered the glasses and looked at her. "Tal…what was wrong with his face?"

She still didn't answer, and there was a weird light in her eyes.

"What?" I asked.

But she didn't need to answer.

Farris said, "Holy fuck!"

I whirled around. The civvie was thirty yards away. Close enough to see him.

Close enough to see.

The kid was walking right toward the bridge, head up now. Eyes on us.

His face…

I thought it was smeared with blood.

But that wasn't it.

He didn't have a face.

Beside me, Joe Bob said, "Wha—wha—wha—?" He couldn't even finish the word.

Farris made a gagging sound. Or maybe that was me.

The civvie kid kept walking straight toward us. Twenty yards. His mouth was open, and for a stupid minute, I thought he was speaking. But you need lips to speak. And a tongue. All he had was teeth. The rest of the flesh on his face was—gone.

Just gone.

Torn away. Or…

Eaten away.

"Jesus Christ, Sal," gasped Talia. "What the fuck? I mean—what the *fuck?*"

Joe Bob swung his big M249 up and dropped the bipod legs on the top sandbag. "I can drop that freak right—"

"Hold your goddamn fire," I growled, and the command in my own voice steadied my feet on the ground. "Farris, Talia—hit the line, but nobody fires a shot unless I say so."

They all looked at me.

"Right fucking now," I bellowed.

They jumped. Farris and Talia brought up their M4 carbines. So did I. The kid was ten yards away now, and he didn't look like he wanted to stop.

"How's he even walking with all that?" asked Talia in a small voice.

I yelled at the civvie. "Hey! Sir? Sir…? I need you to stop right there."

His head jerked up a little more. He had no nose at all. And both eyes were bloodshot and wild. He kept walking, though.

"Sir! Stop. Do not approach the barricade."

He didn't stop.

Then everyone was yelling at him. Ordering him to stop. Telling him to stand down, or lie down, or kneel. Confusing, loud, conflicting. We yelled at the top of our voices as the kid walked right at us.

"I can take him," said Joe Bob in a trembling voice. Was it fear or was he getting ready to bust a nut at the thought of squeezing that trigger?

The civvie was right there. Right in our faces.

He hit the chest-high stack of sandbags and made a grab for me with his bloody fingers. I jumped back.

There was a sudden, three-shot *rat-a-tat-tat*.

The civvie flew back from the sandbags, and the world seemed to freeze as the echoes of those three shots bounced off the bridge and the trees on either side of the river and off the flower water beneath us. Three drum-hits of sound.

I stared at the shooter.

Not Joe Bob. He was as dumbfounded as me.

Talia's face was white with shock at what she had just done.

"Oh...god..." she said, in a voice that was almost no voice at all. Tiny, lost.

Farris and I were in motion in the next second, both of us scrambling over the barricade. Talia stood with her smoking rifle pointed at the sky. Joe Bob gaped at her.

I hit the blacktop and rushed over to where the kid lay sprawled on the ground.

The three-shot burst had caught him in the center of the chest, and the impact had picked him up and dropped him five feet back. His shirt was torn open over a ragged hole.

"Ah...Christ," I said under my breath, and I probably said it forty times as we knelt down.

"We're up the creek on this," said Farris, low enough so Talia couldn't hear.

Behind us, though, she called out, "Is he okay? Please tell me he's okay."

You could have put a beer can in the hole in his chest. Meat and bone were ripped apart; he'd been right up against the barrel when she'd fired.

The kid's eyes were still open.

Wide open.

Almost like they were looking right at…

The dead civvie came up off the ground and grabbed Farris by the hair.

Farris screamed and tried to pull back. I think I just blanked out for a second. I mean…this was impossible. Guy had a fucking hole in his chest and no face and…

Talia and Joe Bob screamed, too.

Then the civvie clamped his teeth on Farris's wrist.

I don't know what happened next. I lost it. We all lost it. One second I was kneeling there, watching Farris hammer at the teenager's face with one fist while blood shot up from between the bastard's teeth. I blinked, and then suddenly the kid was on the ground and the four of us—all of us—were in a circle around him, stomping the shit out of him. Kicking and stamping down and grinding on his bones.

The kid didn't scream.

And he kept twisting and trying to grab at us. With broken fingers, and shattered bones in his arms, he kept reaching. With his teeth kicked out, he kept trying to bite. He would not stop.

We would not stop.

None of us could.

And then Farris grabbed his M4 with bloody hands and fired down at the body as the rest of us leapt back. Farris had it on three-round burst mode. His finger jerked over and over on the trigger and he burned through an entire magazine in a couple of seconds. Thirty rounds. The rounds chopped into the kid. They ruined him. They tore his chest and stomach apart. They blew off his left arm. The tore away what was left of his face.

Farris was screaming.

He dropped the magazine and went to swap in a new one and then I was in his face. I shoved him back.

"*Stop it!*" I yelled as loud as I could.

Farris staggered and fell against the sandbags, and I was there with him, my palms on his chest, both of us staring holes into each other, chests heaving, ears ringing from the gunfire. His rifle dropped to the blacktop and fell over with a clatter.

The whole world was suddenly quiet. We could hear the run of water in the river, but all of the birds in the trees had shut up.

Joe Bob made a small mewling sound.

I looked at him.

He was looking at the kid.

So I looked at the kid, too.

He was a ragdoll, torn and empty.

The son of a bitch was still moving.

"No," I said.

But the day said: *yes.*

-3-

We stood around it.

Not him. *It.*

What else would you call something like this?

"He…can't still be alive," murmured Talia. "That's impossible."

It was like the fifth or sixth time she'd said that.

No one argued with her.

Except the kid was still moving. He had no lower jaw and his half of his neck tendons were shot away, but he kept trying to raise his head. Like he was still trying to bite.

Farris clapped a hand to his mouth and tried not to throw up…but why should he be any different? He spun off and vomited onto the road. Joe Bob and Talia puked in the weeds.

Talia turned away and stood behind Farris, her hand on his back. She bent low to say something to him, but he kept shaking his head.

"What the hell we going to do 'bout this?" asked Joe Bob.

When I didn't answer, the other two looked at me.

"He's right, Sally," said Talia. "We have to do something. We can't leave him like that."

"I don't think a Band-Aid's going to do much frigging good," I said.

"No," she said, "we have to—you know—put him out of his misery."

I gaped at her. "What, you think I'm packing Kryptonite bullets? You shot him and he didn't die, and Farris…Christ, look at this son of a bitch. What the hell do you think *I'd* be able to—"

Talia got up and strode over to me and got right up in my face.

"Do something," she said coldly.

I wasn't backing down because there was nowhere to go. "Like fucking *what*?"

Her eyes held mine for a moment and then she turned, unslung her rifle, put the stock to her shoulder, and fired a short burst into the civvie's head.

If I hadn't hurled my lunch a few minutes ago, I'd have lost it now. The kid's head just flew apart.

Blood and gray junk splattered everyone.

Farris started to cry.

The thunder of the burst rolled past us, and the breeze off the river blew away the smoke.

The civvie lay dead.

Really dead.

I looked at Talia. "How—?"

There was no bravado on her face. She was white as a sheet, and half a step from losing her shit. "What else was there to shoot?" she demanded.

-4-

I called it in.

We were back on our side of the sandbags. The others hunkered down around me.

The kid lay where he was.

Lieutenant Bell said, "You're sure he stopped moving after taking a headshot?"

I'm not sure what I expected the loot to say, but that wasn't it. That was a mile down the wrong road from the right kind of answer. I think I'd have felt better if he reamed me out or threatened some kind of punishment. That, at least, would make sense.

"Yes, sir," I said. "He, um, did not seem to respond to body shots or other damage."

I left him a big hole so he could come back at me on this. I wanted him to.

Instead, he said, "We're hearing this from other posts. Headshots seem to be the only thing that takes these things down."

"Wait, wait," I said, "What do you mean, 'these things'? This was just a kid."

"No," he said. There was a rustling sound and I could tell that he was moving, and when he spoke again, his voice was hushed. "Sal, listen to me here. The shit is hitting the fan. Not just here, but everywhere."

"What shit? What the hell's going on?"

"They…don't really know. All they're saying is that it's spreading like crazy. Western Pennsylvania, Maryland, parts of Virginia and Ohio. It's all over, and people are acting nuts. We've been getting some crazy-ass reports."

"Come on, Loot," I said—and I didn't like the pleading sound in my own voice. "Is this some kind of disease or something?"

"Yes," he said, then, "Maybe. We don't know. *They* don't know, or if they do, then they're sure as shit not telling us."

"But—"

"The thing is, Sally, you got to keep your shit tight. You hear me? You blockade that bridge and I don't care who shows up—nobody gets across. I don't care if it's a nun with an orphan or a little girl with her puppy, you put them down."

"Whoa, wait a frigging minute," I barked, and everyone around me jumped. "What the hell are you saying?"

"You heard me. That kid you put down was infected."

The others were listening to this and their faces looked sick and scared. Mine must have, too.

"Okay," I said, "so maybe he was infected, but I'm not going to open up on everyone who comes down the road. That's crazy."

"It's an order."

"Bullshit. No one's going to give an order like that. No disrespect here, *Lieutenant,* but are you fucking high?"

"That's the order, now follow it…"

"No way. I don't believe it. You can put me up on charges, Loot, but I am not going to—"

"Hey!" snapped Bell. "This isn't a goddamn debate. I gave you an order and—"

"And I don't believe it. Put the captain on the line, or come here with a signed order from him or someone higher, but I'm not going to death row because you're suddenly losing your shit."

The line went dead.

We sat there and stared at each other.

Ferris rubbed his fingers over the bandage Talia had used to dress his bite. His eyes were jumpy.

"What's going on?" he asked. It sounded like a simple question, but we all knew that it wasn't. That question was a tangle of all sorts of barbed wire and broken junk.

I got up and walked over to the wall of sandbags.

We'd stacked them two deep and chest high, but suddenly it felt as weak as a little picket fence. We still had a whole stack of empty bags we hadn't filled yet. We didn't think we'd need to, and they were heavy as shit. I nudged them with the toe of my boot.

I didn't even have to ask. Suddenly we were all filling the bags and building the wall higher and deeper. In the end, we used every single bag.

"Sal," called Talia, holding up the walkie-talkie, "the Loot's calling."

I took it from her, but it wasn't Lieutenant Bell, and it wasn't the captain, either.

"Corporal Tucci?" said a gruff voice that I didn't recognize.

"Yes, sir, this is Tucci."

"This is Major Bradley."

Farris mouthed, *Oh shit.*

"Sir!" I said, and actually straightened like I was snapping to attention.

"Lieutenant Bell expressed your concerns over the orders he gave you."

Here it comes, I thought. *I'm dead or I'm in Leavenworth.*

"Sir, I—"

"I understand your concerns, Corporal," he said. "Those concerns are natural; they show compassion and an honorable adherence to the spirit of who we are as soldiers of this great nation."

Talia rolled her eyes and mimed shoveling shit, but the Major's opening salvo was scaring me. It felt like a series of jabs before an overhand right.

"But we are currently faced with extraordinary circumstances that are unique in my military experience," continued Major Bradley. "We are confronted by a situation in which our fellow citizens are the enemy."

"Sir, I don't—"

He cut me off. "Let me finish, Corporal. You need to hear this."

"Yes, sir. Sorry, sir."

He cleared his throat. "We are facing a biological threat of an unknown nature. It is very likely a terrorist weapon of some kind, but quite frankly, we don't know. What we do know is that the infected are a serious threat. They are violent, they are mentally deranged, and they will attack anyone with whom they come into contact, regardless of age, sex, or any other consideration. We have reports of small children attacking grown men. Anyone who is infected becomes violent. Old people, pregnant women…it, um…doesn't seem to matter." Bradley faltered for a moment, and I wondered if the first part of what he'd said was repeated from orders *he* got and now he was on his own. We all waited.

And waited.

Finally, I said, "Sir?"

But there was no answer.

I checked the walkie-talkie. It was functioning, but Major Bradley had stopped transmitting.

"What the hell?" I said.

"Maybe there's interference," suggested Joe Bob.

I looked around. "Who's got a cell?"

We all had cell phones.

We all called.

I called my brother Vinnie in Newark.

"Sal—Christ on a stick, have you seen the news?" he growled. "Everyone's going ape-shit."

"SAL!"

I spun around and saw Talia pointing past the sandbags.

"They're coming!"

They.

God. They.

The road was thick with them.

Maybe forty. Maybe fifty.

All kinds of them.

Guys in suits. Women in skirts and blouses. Kids. A diner waitress in a pink uniform. A man dressed in surgical scrubs. People.

Just people.

Them.

They didn't rush us.

They *walked* down the road toward the bridge. I think that was one of the worst parts of it. I might have been able to deal with a bunch of psychos running at me. That would have felt like an attack. You see a mob running bat-shit at you and you switch your M4s to rock'n'roll and hope that all of them are right with Jesus.

But they walked.

Walked.

Badly. Some of them limped. I saw one guy walking on an ankle that you could see was broken from fifty yards out. It was buckled over to the side, but he didn't give a shit. There was no wince, no flicker on his face.

The whole bunch of them were like that. None of them looked right. They were bloody. They were ragged.

They were mauled.

"God almighty," whispered Farris.

Talia began saying a Hail Mary.

I heard Joe Bob saying, "Fuck yeah, fuck yeah, fuck yeah." But something in his tone didn't sell it for me. His face was greasy with sweat and his eyes were jumpier than a speed freak's.

The crowd kept coming to us. I'd had to hang up on Vinnie.

"They're going to crawl right over these damn sandbags," complained Farris. The bandage around his wrist was soaked through with blood.

"What do we do?" asked Farris.

He already knew.

When they were fifteen yards away, we opened up.

We burned through at least a mag each before we remembered about shooting them in the head.

Talia screamed it first, and then we were all screaming it. "The head! Shoot for the head!"

"Switch to semi-auto," I hollered. "Check your targets, conserve your ammo."

We stood in a line, our barrels flashing and smoking, spitting fire at the people as they crowded close.

They went down.

Only if we took them in the head. Only then.

At that range, though, we couldn't miss. They walked right up to the barrels. They looked at us as we shot them.

"Jesus, Sal," said Talia as we swapped our mags, "Their eyes. Did you see their eyes?"

I didn't say anything. I didn't have to. When someone is walking up to you and not even ducking away from the shot, you see everything.

We burned through three-quarters of our ammunition.

The air stank of smoke and blood.

Farris was the last one to stop shooting. He was laughing as he clicked on empty, but when he looked back at the rest of us, we could see that there were tears pouring down his cheeks.

The smoke clung to the moment, and for a while, that's all I could see. My mouth was a thick paste of cordite and dry spit. When the breeze came up off the river, we stared into the reality of what we had just done.

"They were all sick, right?" asked Talia. "I mean…they were all infected, right? All of them?"

"Yeah," I said, but what the hell did I know?

We stood there for a long time. None of us knew what the hell to do.

Later, when I tried to call the Major again, I got nothing.

The same thing with the cells. I couldn't even get a signal.

None of us could.

"Come on," I said after a while, "check your ammo."

We did. We had two magazines each, except for Farris, who had one.

Two mags each.

It didn't feel like it was going to be enough.

Talia grabbed my sleeve. "What the hell do we do?"

They all looked at me. Like I knew what the fuck was what.

"We hold this fucking bridge," I said.

No more of them came down the road.

Not then.

Not all afternoon.

Couple of times we heard—or thought we heard—gunfire from way upriver. Never lasted long.

The sun started to fall behind the trees, and it smeared red light over everything. Looked like the world was on fire. I saw Talia staring at the sky for almost fifteen minutes.

"What?" I asked.

"Planes," she said.

I looked up. Way high in the sky there were some contrails, but the sky was getting too dark to see what they were. Something flying in formation, though.

Joe Bob was on watch, and he was talking to himself. Some Bible stuff. I didn't want to hear what it was.

Instead, I went to the Jersey side of the bridge and looked up and down the road. Talia and Farris came with me, but there was nothing to see.

"Maybe they made a public service announcement," said Talia. "Like the Emergency Broadcast Network thing. Maybe they told everyone to stay home, stay off the roads."

"Sure," I said in pretty much the same way you'd say 'bullshit'.

We watched the empty road as the sky grew darker.

"We could just leave," said Farris. "Head up the road. There's that Quizno's. Maybe we can find a ride."

"We can't leave the bridge," I said.

"Fuck the bridge."

I got up in his face. "Really? You want to let *them* just stroll across the bridge? Is that your plan? Is that what you think will get the job done?"

"What job? We're all alone out here. Might as well have been on the far side of the goddamn moon."

"They'll come back for us," I said. "You watch; in the morning there'll be a truck with supplies, maybe some hot coffee."

"Sure," he said, in exactly the same way I had a minute ago.

-8-

That night, there were a million stars and a bright three-quarter moon. Plenty of light to see the road. Only one of them came down the road. Talia was on watch and she took it down with a single shot to the head. She let the thing—it used to be a mailman—walk right up to the sandbags. It opened its mouth, even though it was too far away to bite, and Talia shot it in the eye.

Then she sat down and cried like a little girl for ten whole minutes. I stood her watch and let her cry. I wished I could do that. For me, it was all stuck inside and it was killing me that I couldn't let it go.

-9-

Farris got sick in the night.

I heard him throwing up, and I came over and shined my flashlight on him. His face was slick with sweat. Joe Bob went back to the wall and Talia knelt next to me. She knew more First Aid than I did, and she took Farris's vitals as best she could.

"Wow, he's burning up," she said, looking at his fever-bright eyes and sweaty face, but then she put her palm on his forehead and frowned. "That's weird. He's cold."

"Shock?" I asked, but she didn't answer.

Then she examined the bite and I heard her gasp. When I shined my light on Farris's arm, I had to bite my lip. The wound on Farris's wrist was bad enough, but there were weird black lines running all the way up his arm. It was like someone had used a Sharpie to outline every vein and capillary.

"It's infection," said Talia, but I knew that it was worse than that.

"God," gasped Farris, "it's blood poisoning."

I said nothing, because I thought it was worse than that, too. Even in the harsh glare of the flashlight, his color looked weird.

Talia met my eyes over the beam of the light. She didn't say anything, but we had a whole conversation with that one look.

I patted Farris on the shoulder. "You get some sleep, man. In the morning we'll get a medic down here to give you a shot, set you right."

Fear was jumping up in his eyes. "You sure? They can give me something for this?"

"Yeah. Antibiotics and shit."

Talia fished in her first-aid kit. There was a morphine curette. She showed it to me and I nodded.

"Sweet dreams, honey," she said as she jabbed Farris with the little needle. His eyes held hers for a moment, and then he was out.

We made sure he was comfortable and then we got up and began walking up and down the length of the bridge. Talia kept looking up at the moon.

"Pretty night," I said.

She made a face.

"*Should* be a pretty night," I amended.

We stopped for a moment and looked down at the rushing water. It was running fast and high after that big storm a couple of days ago, and each little wave-tip gleamed with silver moonlight. Maybe fifteen, twenty minutes passed while we stood there, our shoulders a few inches apart, hands on the cold metal rail, watching the river do what rivers do.

"Sally?" she asked softly.

"Yeah?"

"This is all happening, right?"

I glanced at her. "What do you mean?"

She used her fingers to lightly trace circles on the inside of her forearm. "You know I used to ride the spike, right? I mean, that's not news."

"I figured."

"I've been getting high most of my life. Since…like seventh grade. Used to swipe pills from my mom's purse. She did a lot of speed, so that's what I started on. Rode a lot of fast waves, y'know?"

"Yeah." I was never much of a hophead, but I lived in Newark and I'd seen a lot of my friends go down in flames.

"Until I got clean the last time, I was probably high more than I was on the ground."

I said nothing.

"So," she continued, "I seen a lot of weird shit. While I was jonesing for a hit, while I was high, on the way down. You lose touch, y'know?"

"Yeah."

"People talk about pink elephants and polka-dotted lobsters and shit, but that's not what comes out of the woodwork." She shivered and gripped the rail with more force. Like it was holding her there. "And not a day goes by—not a fucking day—when I don't want a fix. Even now, twenty-three months clean, I can feel it. It's like worms crawling under my skin. That morphine? You think I haven't dreamed about that every night?"

I nodded. "My Uncle Tony's been in and out of twelve steps for booze. I've seen how he looks at Thanksgiving when the rest of us are drinking beers and watching the ball game. Like he'd take a knife to any one of us for a cold bottle of Coors."

"Right. Did your uncle ever talk to you about having a dry drunk? About feeling stoned and even seeing the spiders come crawling out of the sofa when he hasn't even had a drop?"

"Couple times."

"I get that," she said. "I get that a lot."

I waited.

"That's why I need you to tell me that this is all really happening; or am I lost inside my own head?"

I turned to her and touched her arm. "I wish to Christ and the baby Jesus that I could say that you're just tripping. Having a dry drunk, or whatever you'd call it. A flashback—whatever. But…I ain't a drunk and I never shot up, and here I am, right with you. Right here in the middle of this shit."

Talia closed her eyes and leaned her forehead on the backs of the hands that clung so desperately to the rail. "Ah…fuck," she said quietly.

I felt like a total asshole for telling her the truth.

Then Talia stiffened, and I saw that she was looking past her hands. "What's that?"

"What?"

She pointed over the rail. "In the water. Is that a log, or…?"

Something bobbed up and down as the current swept it toward the bridge. It looked black in the moonlight, but as it came closer we could see that part of it was white.

The face.

White.

We stared at it…and it stared back up at us.

Its mouth was open, working, like it was trying to bite us even as the river pulled it under the bridge and then out the other side. We hurried to the other side and stared over, watching the thing reach toward us, its white fingers clawing the air.

Then it was gone. A shape, then a dot, then nothing.

Neither of us could say a word.

Until the next one floated by. And the next.

"God, no…" whispered Talia.

We went back to the other side of the bridge.

"There's another," I said. "No…two…no…"

I stopped counting.

Counting didn't matter.

Who cares how many of them floated down? Two, three hundred? A thousand?

After the first one, really, who cared how many?

Talia and I stood there all night, watching. There were ordinary civilians and people in all kinds of uniforms. Cops, firemen, paramedics. Soldiers. I wished to God that I had a needle of heroin for her. And for me.

We didn't tell the others.

-10-

I'm not sure what time the bodies stopped floating past. The morning was humid and there was a thick mist. It covered the river, and maybe there were still bodies down there, or maybe the fog hid them.

We stood there as the fog curled gray fingers around the bridge and pulled itself up to cover everything. The wall of sandbags, Joe Bob, the sleeping figure of Farris, our gear. All of it.

Talia and I never moved from the rail, even when it got hard to see each other.

"They'll come for us, right?" she asked. "The Lieutenant? The supply truck? They'll come to get us, right?"

"Absolutely," I said. She was a ghost beside me.

"You're sure?"

"They'll come."

And they did.

It wasn't long, either, but the sun was already up and the fog was starting to thin out. Talia saw them first and she stiffened.

"Sally…"

I turned to look.

At first it was only a shape. A single figure, and my heart sank. It came down the road from the direction our truck had come, walking wearily toward us from the Jersey side. In the fog it was shapeless, shambling.

Talia whimpered, just a sound of denial that didn't have actual words.

"Fuck me," I whispered, but before I could even bring my gun up, the fog swirled and I could see the mishmash stripes of camouflage, the curve of a helmet, the sharp angles of a rifle on its sling.

Talia grabbed my arm. "Sally? Look!"

There was movement behind the soldier, and, one by one, shapes emerged. More camos, more tin pots.

More soldiers.

They came walking down the road. Five of them. Then more.

"It's the whole platoon," Talia said, and laughter bubbled in her voice.

But it was more than that. As the mist thinned, I could see a lot of soldiers. A hundred at least. More.

"Damn," I said, "they look bone-ass tired. They must have been fighting all night."

"Is it over?" she asked. "Have we beaten this goddamn thing?"

I smiled. "I think so."

I waved, but no one waved back. Some of them could barely walk. I could understand, I felt like I could drop where I stood. We'd been up all night watching the river.

"Talia, go wake up Farris and tell Joe Bob to look sharp."

She grinned and spun away and vanished into the veil of fog that still covered the bridge.

I took a second to straighten my uniform and sling my rifle the right way. I straightened my posture and stepped off the bridge onto the road, looking tough, looking like someone who maybe should get some sergeant's stripes for holding this frigging bridge. Army strong, booyah.

I saw Lieutenant Bell, and he was as wrung out as the rest of them. He lumbered through the fog, shoulders slumped, and behind him were gray soldiers. Even from this distance I could tell that no one was smiling. And for a moment I wondered if maybe this was a retreat rather than a surge. Shit. Had they gotten their asses kicked and these were the survivors? If so…Bell would have his ass handed to him and I wouldn't be going up a pay grade.

"Well, whatever," I said to myself. "Fireteam Delta held the bridge, so fuck it and fuck you and hooray for the red, white, and blue."

A breeze wandered out of the south and it blew past me, swirling the mist, blowing it off the bridge and pushing it away from the soldiers. The mass of gray figures changed into khaki and brown and green.

And red.

All of them.

Splashed with…

I turned and screamed at the top of my lungs. "*TALIA! Joe Bob, Farris!* Lock and load. Hostiles on the road…"

The breeze had blown all the mist off of the bridge.

Talia stood forty feet from the wall of sandbags. Her rifle hung from its sling, the sling in her hand, the stock of the weapon on the blacktop. She stood, her back to me, staring at Joe Bob.

At what was left of Joe Bob.

Farris must have heard something. Maybe a sound I made, or Talia's first scream. He froze in the midst of lifting something from Joe Bob's stomach. Some piece of something. I couldn't tell what, didn't care what.

Farris bared his teeth at us.

Then he stuffed the thing into his mouth and chewed.

Where he wasn't covered with blood, Farris's skin was gray-green and veined with black lines.

Behind me I heard the shuffling steps of the soldiers as the first of them left the road and stepped onto the bridge.

Talia turned toward me, and in her eyes I saw everything that had to be in my own eyes.

Her fingers twitched and the rifle dropped to the asphalt.

"Please," she said. Her mouth trembled into a smile. "Please."

Please.

I raised my rifle, racked the bolt, and shot her. She was never a pretty girl. Too thin, too worn by life. She had nice eyes, though, and a nice smile. The bullets took that away, and she fell back.

I heard—*felt*—someone come up behind me.

Some*thing.*

Probably Bell.

I turned. I still only had two mags. Less three bullets.

There were hundreds of them.

I raised my rifle.

--The End--

You'll Never Be Lunch in This Town Again

Dana Fredsti

First time director Darren Zuber was having a hard enough time shooting his film *before* the dead started coming back to life and eating the living.

Mara Dubray, his leading lady and a well-known star of daytime soaps, was proof positive that most actors' IQs and egos were inversely proportional. Known more for her enormous bosom rather than any real acting talent, Mara was not about to let some first-time director tell *her* how to deliver lines. Her tantrums had already run the film well over budget and the words "completion bond company" had been bandied about more than once by Gerald Fife, the executive producer.

Never mind that it had been Fife's brilliant idea to cast a mediocre soap star as Lady Genevieve, a noblewoman in love with a priest (played by Derrick Stone, a minor name whose entire range consisted of stoically wooden) in the midst of a plague-stricken 14th Century Europe.

Darren had fought this casting — certainly the most ludicrous decision since Verhoven had cast Melanie Griffith as Elizabeth I ("I have the mind of a king and a bod made for sin") as vehemently as he dared. But with only a music video directing credit under his belt, Darren had to swallow both pride and common sense on a great many crucial details, such as casting and rewrites. It was the only way to get his film made, a project he'd dreamed of doing since his first years at UCLA. And it was only the success of *Game of Thrones* that had convinced Plateau Productions, headed by Fife, to invest the money.

Plateau was known for low-budget rip-offs of big box office pictures, as well as micro-budget exploitation films in every genre. If you rented a Plateau picture you could always count on four things: bad scripts, worse acting, one or two minor "name" actors for foreign draw, and at least one scene set in a strip club.

Explanations to Five that 14th century Europeans did not have strip clubs were useless. To Fife, if a film didn't have topless dancers, it wasn't a film. "You gotta have tits and ass, kid," Fife had said during one of their many rewrite sessions. "And I don't give a shit what century we're talking here; you can't tell me that the men didn't want to see naked girls after a hard day plowing in the field, even if they hadn't invented boob jobs yet." Darren had given in, figuring he could come up with some sort of scene in a tavern with bawdy serving maids and a band of roving minstrels for the music.

But it was certainly a far cry from the idealism of film school and all of those vows Darren and his fellow students had made. *They* would never sell out to the commercialism of Hollywood. Their movies would be pure; art for art's sake. No stars (unless it was an older name, like Maureen O'Hara or a 80s sitcom star. Both had a certain cache that appealed to the idealistic — and pretentious — students in the UCLA film program); no more than one explosion per film, and *no* scripts by Roland Emmerich.

Darren wondered how many film school grads had their idealism kicked out of them by the steel-toed boots of companies like Plateau. He supposed he should be grateful to have won the battle against a rock'n'roll soundtrack.

As he stared balefully at Mara while she finished butchering yet another speech, however, Darren found it hard to be grateful about anything.

The scene would have to be done again to get the master shot, and then there would be countless takes on key phrases, close-ups, reaction shots from the crowd of peasants as Lady Genevieve tried to convince them not to flee their village, and—

Shit! Was one of the extras wearing sunglasses?

Why the hell hadn't the extra coordinator or the wardrobe mistress caught that? And how had *he* missed it? And how could that asshat of an extra be so…so *brain*-dead? Several scenes would now have to be reshot, adding more to the already inflated budget.

Darren groaned and rubbed his head, trying to convince the nagging ache behind one eye that it did *not* want to become a migraine. Melissa, his assistant, silently handed him two Excedrin Migraine and an unopened can of soda. Darren mouthed a silent "thanks" and popped the top, washing down the pills with a mouthful of sickly sweet orange-flavored carbonation.

"Jeez, this stuff is crap." Darren handed the can back to Melissa. "Can't those P.A's get anything but this shit?"

Melissa shrugged. "Budget'll only cover generic. Besides, the whole dead thing back east is really playing havoc with shipments."

"Jesus…" Darren turned to his first A.D. "John, call lunch. We'll take this scene again after that. And tell Zack to make sure none of the extras are wearing fucking sunglasses! Or watches, or any other jewelry, for crissake! These are 14th century peasants! And tell Linda I want more yellow on their teeth! They didn't *have* Crest in the 14th century! Jesus!"

Darren stomped off without waiting for an answer, unable to control his temper. He didn't like losing it in front of people. He had promised himself he wasn't going to be one of those abusive directors famous for their on-set tantrums. But he hadn't bargained for the reality of low-budget Hollywood.

At least Darren didn't have to handle the situation by himself. Thank God for John, a fellow student from UCLA and one of the few people Darren could really count on. His producer, Phil, was another friend from film school. The three of them had shared many a late night pizza while watching The Definitive Movie Masterpieces as defined by their film prof, analyzing them to a degree that would have both amazed and amused the original filmmakers.

John still retained some of the purity of vision they'd once all shared, albeit tempered with an increasingly world-weary attitude now reflected by his newly tinted glasses. Phil, however, had not only happily tossed idealism out the window; he'd also thrown out imagination, courage, and loyalty. He made up for these gaps in his character by extra brown-nosing and sleaziness genes.

Even now, instead of showing any interest in the increasingly disastrous proceedings, Phil was off in a corner schmoozing some buxom peasant girl. Osne wearing a pair of decidedly non-period earrings and far too much self-applied cosmetics, despite strict instructions from the makeup department.

Darren went off in search of something stronger than Excedrin.

The next day brought a whole slew of unpleasant surprises, including the news that Joe Pilate (one of the few actors Darren had actually cast himself) had been eaten the day before. Phil delivered the unpleasant news via telephone before Darren had a chance to sip his morning espresso.

"Eaten? What the hell do you mean, 'he was eaten?'"

"Had his guts ripped right out," Phil confirmed with ghoulish relish. "Joe was visiting his father's grave in Philly and a couple of deadheads had him for lunch."

"Jesus, that's sick." Darren was dismayed that even while he mourned the death of a friend, his mind was already going over possible replacements for the devoured actor.

"That's the east coast for you," Phil said. "By the way, Fife is really on my ass about the budget. Are there any more scenes we can cut?"

Darren swore. It would already take an editing genius to make a coherent story out of the amputated bits left from his original script. Not for the first time, he suspected Fife had a sympathetic ear in Phil.

"Forget it," he growled. "Any more cuts and we're going to have a 14th century music video."

"Hey, we could get a rock band and have them do a title song," Phil said enthusiastically. "Call it *Plague Years* or something!"

Darren closed his eyes. "I'm going to pretend I didn't hear that. Bottom line, no more cuts." He paused, finding his next words sticking in his throat. "And find me a replacement for Joe ASAP. We'll shift his scenes to Thursday. I'll have Melissa call the actors and let 'em know we're doing the love scene today."

Hanging up before Phil could argue, Darren sadly reflected that he'd just given Joe an extremely shoddy obituary.

As soon as he arrived on set, Melissa told Darren that Mara was refusing to do the love scene with Derrick unless provided with a bottle of Cristal to relax her.

"Relax her?" Phil, who had joined the pair as they walked towards the craft service table, snorted in derision. "If she'd lay off the coke or whatever other crap she's been taking, she'd relax just fine."

"I don't know." Melissa shrugged fatalistically; something she'd been doing a lot the past few days. "She says the whole dead coming back to life thing is really stressing her out."

"Oh, that's a load of crap," Phil snarled, grabbing a bagel and slathering it with cream cheese. "This is Hollywood, not

Philadelphia."

Darren headed straight for the Excedrin.

"I don't know." Melissa shrugged again, pouring herself a cup of coffee. "They're saying it's spreading."

"'They?' Who are 'they', Mara? That's total bullshit." Phil bit viciously into his bagel. "She just wants to get loaded on good champagne on our dime."

"I guess," Melissa said doubtfully. "So what should I tell her?"

Darren sighed, deciding he'd better step in. "Get some Tott's or Korbel and don't let her see the bottle. I doubt she'll know the difference. She only knows about Cristal because she's watched *Showgirls* at least twenty times."

Later, as he tried to coax some genuine emotion out of his two leads, Darren reflected that if the walking dead problem *did* spread out west, no one would be able to tell the difference between the zombies and his actors anyway, so who'd give a shit?

The next day, both the media and the general uproar in the city confirmed the fact that, like practically everyone else in the country, the dead had indeed migrated to the west coast. Traffic was abysmal; it took Darren two hours to drive from Culver City to the studio in Burbank. He wasn't sure, but he thought several of the scruffy street people he passed on the way looked…well…*dead.*

At the studio, for the first time Darren could remember, the large electronic iron gates were shut, a heavily armed security guard screening each new arrival very carefully before letting them in. Another guard, also packing what looked to be a heavy-caliber weapon, kept vigilant watch each time the gates opened and closed.

Melissa greeted Darren with the news that several crewmembers (two production assistants and a grip) were missing. They hadn't called in. They were just … missing. "And we're short extras too," Melissa added. "Central Casting called and said a bunch of their people are afraid to drive anywhere."

John walked up, radio in hand. "I figure we'll have to do tighter shots to get the kind of crowd effect you want with the plague victims."

Darren set his mouth in a determined line. "Let's just do it."

He stalked towards the day's first set; the interior of a church where several hundred plague victims, both dead and dying, were gathered to seek salvation. About seventy-five extras, gruesomely made up to look like they were in the final throes of the Black Death, were sitting in the aisles and rough-hewn wooden pews, nervously discussing the more current plague of ravenous corpses. The crew looked equally distracted. Very few were actually doing their jobs.

Darren thought they'd have to do some fast-talking to keep people on the film so he called a meeting with John and Phil.

"So what do you think?" he said after outlining his concerns.

"I just don't know, Darren," Phil replied. "I mean, you've got people scared to leave their homes. Businesses are shutting down. I mean, *Starbucks* was closed this morning." He stared at both Darren and John in turn. "*Star*bucks."

"Do what you can," Darren said, trying not to imagine a world without readily available coffee. "Offer bonus pay, whatever it takes."

"*Bonus* pay?" Phil sounded outraged. "Are you nuts? Do you know what Fife will say if I do that?"

"Don't tell him!" Darren slammed his hand against a chair

in frustration. "Jesus, Phil, there's got to be something we can do!"

Phil was quiet – a sign that his mind was working furiously. After a moment of reflection he smiled broadly. "I've got it!" He lowered his voice. "We'll *offer* the bonus pay. But we don't have to actually *pay* them the extra money."

John nodded thoughtfully.

Darren, on the other hand, was horrified, both at the idea and John's calm reaction to it. "Jesus, Phil, that's totally unethical! These people are working their asses off!"

"Yeah, and we're paying them. There aren't any clauses in their contracts for a zombie plague."

"Look, Phil, they have every reason to demand more money if they're risking their lives to be here."

John nodded. "He's got a point, Phil. You know how much stuntmen get paid."

Phil brought his face close to Darren's. "Do you want to finish this film or not?"

John nodded again. "He's got a point, Darren."

Thousands of objections whirled around in Darren's mind, but all he could come up with was a feeble, "But we could get sued!"

Phil shrugged. "Yeah, maybe. But with all this other shit going down, who's gonna have time to deal with it?"

John shook his head doubtfully. "SAG isn't going to let a little thing like zombies stop them from fucking with the production if we screw their actors over, you know that. And the Teamsters…"

The three men shook their heads, differences momentarily forgotten as they contemplated the eternal enemy of the low-budget filmmaker: the Unions.

Taking advantage of the moment of camaraderie, Phil rested his hand on Darren's shoulder. "Let's get this film finished, buddy. This is what we worked for in film school, right? So we'll do whatever we have to do."

Darren felt a tiny piece of his soul die as he heard himself reply, "You got it."

The offer of hazard pay got about two-thirds of the cast and crew on set the next day. Darren had sympathetic for the absentees. The commute to the studio had been even worse than the previous day.

He'd definitely seen people—both living and dead—with large chunks missing from various limbs, all staggering around the streets. The kind of stuff nightmares were made of.

On the other hand, it was a definite solution to the homeless problem.

Darren's main concern was the number of armed soldiers and national guardsmen now patrolling the city. Certain broadcasts on radio and TV said the government was planning to impose a twenty-four hour curfew on the streets. That would make it impossible to get to and from the studio. Darren had brought an overnight bag just in case and had called to tell Phil and Melissa to do the same.

Melissa had been charged with the duty of calling as many other crew and cast members as she could reach and suggest they plan on staying over too. "People aren't going to want to leave their families," Melissa had pointed out when asked to make the call.

"They can bring their families with them," Darren had immediately replied.

Darren was gratified to see some people actually did bring their families (and pets) with them to the studio. When Phil pointed out this would compensate for the shortage of extras, Darren agreed, thinking it would keep their minds off the horrors outside of the studio walls.

Today was a key scene. Lady Genevieve accidentally reveals her love for the handsome priest in front of the townspeople when she seeks him out in the church so he can read the Last Rites over her dying father.

The scene was shot several times before lunch, Mara doing an abysmal job of conveying any real emotion. Whether she was trying to show fear, love, hate or indifference, Mara just looked as though she had a bad case of gas.

"I can't concentrate!" she wailed when Darren didn't bother to hide his impatience with her lack of talent. "There are *dead* people outside!"

"Well, they're not *inside*," Darren shot back coldly. "And they aren't paying your salary." He turned away, dismissing her before he said something he really regretted. "Now people, we're going to break for lunch and then try this again. The caterer did show up, didn't he?"

When Mara didn't return to set after lunch, Darren assumed she was throwing a tantrum because he hadn't treated her with the respect she didn't deserve. Everyone else was in place, waiting for the camera to roll. Derrick, playing the handsome young priest stood patiently at the pulpit, muttering lines that would all come out sounding heroically wooden.

Patience worn paper-thin, Darren stalked towards Mara's trailer, determined to drag her out by her hair if need be.

"Damn it, I hate actors," he muttered, rapping sharply on the trailer door with a closed fist. When no response was forthcoming Darren threw manners to the wind and flung the door open hard enough to send it smacking into the inside wall.

"Mara, get your ass out here! I swear, I'm going to make sure you never work in this town again if you don't stop this shit!" Aware that he'd just made an empty threat, Darren took the stairs in one long stride and stuck his head around the corner. "Mara, I mean it. I—"

Darren stopped short, confronted by the sight of Mara's prone body, still in 14th century garb, lying on the trailer floor, one hand clutching a hypodermic, the other splayed lifelessly to one side.

"Oh, shit." Darren knelt by his erstwhile leading lady's corpse, taking a quick check on her pulse to see if he might just be wrong.

Nope, absolutely nothing.

Mara was dead.

Darren waited for the rush of grief one was supposed feel at the death of someone…well, not close, but certainly someone he'd worked closely with for several weeks. He was dismayed to discover that amongst his mixed emotions, the strongest was overwhelming annoyance. A new, darker side of Darren reflected that on any other occasion Mara's death might even be a cause for celebration. But now Mara was once again holding up his film.

Darren sat back on his heels.

"Oh, you dumb bitch. How the hell am I going to shoot around you?"

Darren walked slowly back to set, leaving Mara's corpse to be disposed of after he'd figured out how to salvage the film. Body double, using close-ups from previously shot footage? Might just work, although it would be tricky.

Darren joined John, Phil and Melissa by the camera. Correctly reading his expression, Melissa asked, "Trouble?"

"What?" Phil frowned. "She won't come back to set? I'll handle it." Phil strode towards Mara's trailer, obviously confident his powers of persuasion were more than ample for the job at hand.

Darren stopped him with a hand on one shoulder. "She can't come back on set, Phil. She's dead. Mara OD'd."

All three stared at him blankly. Finally Phil shook his head. "Jesus. Fife just isn't going to be happy about this." His voice took on an accusatory tone as he continued, "She was a *big* part of the deal! You know that, Darren!"

Darren's response was forestalled by the appearance of Derrick, their male lead. "Are we going to get going soon, Darren?" The actor wiped sweat from his stoically handsome forehead. "Goddamn lights are melting the makeup off my face and that *always* makes my skin break out."

Darren considered several replies, discarding each one before it made its way from his brain to his mouth. He supposed he'd have to tell people that Mara Dubray was no longer among the living, but—

"Oh, shit."

The actor stared at him. "It's okay, Darren. I'll just see my dermatologist. It shouldn't affect filming or anything."

But Darren wasn't paying attention to Derrick. He was too busy staring over his shoulder as Mara staggered and swayed her way towards them, an expression of intense longing stamped on her face. Her mouth was open slightly, an ululating moan of desire emerging from it, along with a copious stream of drool running down one side of her chin.

"I thought you said she was dead," Phil hissed in a stage whisper.

Darren noted the slightly bluish tint to Mara's skin. "She is dead."

He didn't bother lowering his voice.

Everyone on set stopped what they were doing and now stared at Mara's awkward yet determined progress towards the small group of people by the camera.

As the implications of Darren's comment hit home, Melissa, Phil and John scattered. The clueless Derrick stayed where he was. Darren was too busy watching Mara in fascination to do more than step to one side, leaving the path wide open toward the actor.

Mara's attention focused specifically on her screen lover and she lurched towards him with outstretched arms, fingers opening and closing spasmodically. Before anyone could react, she threw her arms around Derrick with passionate intensity and took a distinctly unlover-like bite out of his well-muscled shoulder.

Chaos ensued as several hefty grips pried a snarling Mara off the screaming actor.

Darren turned to Phil, his face alight with enthusiasm.

"Shit! Did you see that?" he exclaimed. "That's the best acting she's done since we've started. Let's get that on film!"

Darren sat in the screening room watching dailies with Phil, a contented smile on his face. For the first time since filming began he was actually happy with the way Mara played a scene. Granted, some fancy editing would have to be done to replace the look of abject terror on Derrick's face with a look of tormented longing, but that could be done. Come to think of it, it was the most expressive Derrick had ever been as well.

It had taken some doing to restore enough order on set to continue filming. Convincing Derrick to play the scenes had been the hardest part, but an appeal to the actor's vanity, the promise of more money, and the two big grips standing by to prevent a repeat of Mara's first attack had worked wonders. "Besides," Phil had pointed out, "It's not *that* big of a bite." And luckily one of the people who'd made it to the studio that day was the on-set medic.

Darren managed to console his own outraged conscience with this last fact.

The rest of the cast and crew had responded with amazing equanimity, and Darren suspected part of that had to do with needing the work to keep their minds off of what might be happening outside the studio. This thought also made Darren feel better as he watched the dailies.

He made the mistake of mentioning it to Phil, who replied, "Whatever. Just so long as they keep working."

Darren stared at his erstwhile friend in disbelief. "How the hell can you be so callous?" He preferred to forget his own reaction to Mara's death and the subsequent improvement of her acting ability.

"Oh, get off your high horse," Phil retorted. "You've got the best fucking acting you've had since we started so don't get all moralistic on me. A filmmaker's gotta do what a filmmaker's gotta do. It's the art that matters." Phil gestured towards the screen. "I mean, just look at that. It's beautiful!"

Darren looked. It *was* beautiful, damn it. Except for that one moment when Mara's attention turned from Derrick to one of the extras who'd gotten a little too close…

Darren winced at the memory.

He turned to Phil. "We'll have to remember to keep the other actors far enough away to keep Mara's focus on Derrick. It distracts from the intensity of her emotions. And we had a few close calls today that I don't want to repeat."

"Yeah," Phil agreed. "We can't afford to lose any more of our extras. Those crowd scenes look pretty sparse as it is."

"I know," Darren sighed. "But we're not likely to get anyone else from outside so we'll just have to make due with what we've got, add in CGI later."

Phil shook his head. "The only CGI we can afford on our budget will look like crap. Maybe…" He paused and suddenly his eyes brightened. "Oh, man," he said slowly. "Have I got an idea!"

At first Darren had been totally appalled by Phil's brainstorm, delivering an unequivocal "No!" in response. How could Phil even *think* of it? Didn't he understand the moral implications?

"What moral implications?" Phil was genuinely confused by the question. "These people are *dead*, Darren. They're not going to care. Most of them probably wanted to be actors anyway so you'd be doing them a favor. "

Darren's moral outrage sputtered a bit, then flared up again when he thought of new objections. "What about the danger? I mean, catching them in the first place. Who the hell is going to agree to do that?"

"Production assistants," Phil replied calmly. "Tony'd do anything for this film. He'll probably think it's fun. Besides, with the equipment I've got in mind it shouldn't be a problem."

"But what about the danger to the cast and crew?" Darren demanded. "How the hell are we going to handle that?"

"Have the set design folks come up with something to keep 'em separate from the others during the scenes. We can use handcuffs, hide 'em under the costumes."

As Phil proceeded to counter all of Darren's objections with arguments that at least *sounded* reasonable, Darren allowed himself to be persuaded it really would be a *good* idea to use some of the newly ambulatory dead to supplement the crowd scenes.

Somewhere in the back of his mind, a little voice told him he was making a compromise even more Faustian than his deal with Gerald Fife. But the dailies in front of him and Phil's persuasiveness were better than a pair of earplugs. And once committed to the idea, Darren put his considerable energy into implementing it.

Even without the steady stream of media reports (and CNN was over the moon to have something this big to report on without the need to supplement it with brain candy filler), Darren had only to look outside the studio gates to see the situation was definitely worsening. There were more walking dead roaming around the area, lots of cars driving frantically up and down the surface streets, general chaos. Only one of the security guards remained at his post, steadfastly ignoring his erstwhile partner who was now banging on the gates from the outside, a large chunk of flesh missing from the side of his neck.

Darren approached the remaining guard. "You still letting

people in and out of here?"

The guard nodded. "As long as they show their badges."

"Great." Something else occurred to Darren. "Any more guns here?"

"We have a few in the Security office."

"Do you think—"

The guard shook his head. "No way. That's against the law."

Using his most persuasive tone, Darren said, "C'mon—" He looked at the guard's nametag. "C'mon, Arthur. I've got to send some people out on a run and they need protection."

"I don't know…"

Darren played his trump card. "Y'know, I could use you in this film, Arthur. I've lost a couple of my co-stars because of these damn zombies."

The guard tossed Darren a key. "Just don't tell anyone where you got it. It'd be my ass."

Darren walked off to find the security office, thankful that everyone in this town really *did* want to be an actor.

Melissa listened carefully and jotted down notes as Darren gave her the list of items he wanted one of the production assistants to pick up on what might be their only run outside the studio. When he was finished, he had her read the list back to him. Phil stood to one side, nodding his head.

"Okay. Dry ice, lots of it. Any food he can find. The thickest sports padding available. Heavy-duty steel collars. Leather will do, but steel preferable. Chain leashes—" Melissa stopped and looked at both Darren and Phil. "Are you sure about this?"

Phil nodded. "Ought to be a piece of cake."

"Hmm," Melissa said doubtfully. "Okay. John's rifles plus ammo … we're gonna need his house key and directions." She jotted down another notation. "Okay, I think that's just about it."

The on-set medic strode up, her forehead creased with lines of worry. "Are you sending someone outside?"

Darren nodded.

"Good. I need some antibiotics as soon as possible. Derrick isn't looking too good. That bite is festering and it looks like the infection is spreading rapidly beyond the wound."

Melissa made another notation on her list.

A shriek from Mara's trailer drew their attention. Linda, the rather temperamental makeup girl, came running out of it clutching her hand. Her assistant, a mousy little thing whose name no one could ever remember, trailed at her heels.

"Darren!" Linda's voice was raised several notches above her usual petulant whine. "I absolutely cannot work under these conditions! I can only do so much with someone whose skin is naturally blue. And when I tried putting lipstick on her, she bit me!" Linda dramatically held up one hand to show a smallish bite mark. The medic looked at it worriedly.

"Add a mortician's makeup kit to that list," Phil said thoughtfully. "Hell, bring a mortician. Might make more sense and we won't have to pay Union scale."

Linda started to sputter in outrage and Phil snarled, "Listen, Linda. If you can't do your job, I'm going to get someone who can. Give me any shit and you'll be working Craft Services. And I'm not talking about behind the table."
someone used to being ignored.

Darren considered the idea, grateful for even this token safety measure with which to salve his increasingly battered conscience. "Just might work!"

The makeup assistant looked absurdly gratified.

"Darren, it has to look like she's really talking," Phil protested. "How the hell are you going to loop in her dialogue realistically if her mouth doesn't move?"

Darren shot Phil a resentful glance, hating the fact that his producer was right.

"Okay," he amended. "Let's try sewing the corners so she can't get a good bite radius going." Phil nodded his approval and Darren continued, "Melissa, talk to wardrobe and see what they can do."

Turning back to the mousy assistant he said, "Good thinking, honey. Do you think you can do something with Mara's makeup so we can get the next scene shot before we lose the light?"

The assistant nodded, eager to prove her worth. She scurried back to Mara's trailer as a protesting Linda was led off to be treated by the medic.

Darren resumed his conversation with Melissa and Phil. "We can sew the new extras' mouths completely shut. They don't have to talk. And make sure the PA – who are we using?"

Melissa checked her list. "Tony."

"Good. He's smart. Make sure he's got a decent gun."

"Got it." Melissa set off to make sure everything on her list was done with her usual efficiency. Then she stopped and turned back. "Darren, shouldn't we send someone to ride shotgun with Tony? They'd stand a better chance of getting back safely."

"Phil, can we spare the extra hand or—" Darren stopped abruptly. "Jesus, I don't believe I said that. Of course we can spare someone else. Whatever it takes to bring them back safely."

"And more quickly," Phil agreed. "It'd be hell to try and find more good production assistants."

Darren ignored that. "Okay, let's get moving."

"Yeah," Phil said. "We should get going on Derrick's death scene while he's still got some life in him."

The scene went well. Derrick shivered with a real fever no amount of acting -- at least on *his* part -- could emulate. His skin was pasty, sweat poured off of him in rivulets, and he seemed to be suffering from as much pain as a plague victim in the last stages of bubonic plague would have felt. Darren was delighted with the results.

On a purely artistic level, of course.

The medic stood at the sidelines throughout, wearing an expression that alternated between disapproval and downright horror. She had vehemently protested the decision to shoot a scene with the sick man but Derrick himself had insisted. He was a professional, by God, and he would act as long as he could breathe -- state lasting approximately ten minutes after they finished shooting his death scene.

Darren immediately had someone from Wardrobe stitch the dead actor's lips partially shut, consoling himself with the thought that he'd given Derrick the chance to die with his acting boots on, so to speak.

"You are using buttonhole thread, aren't you?" he asked the woman pushing a needle in and out of Derrick's lips.

She looked up in annoyance. "Please. I *do* know my job."

Several hours later the production assistants returned from their run, loaded down with all the items on their list, including a dozen large coolers full of dry ice, several intimidating rifles, and a star-struck mortician. The mortician was sent off to see what he could do with Mara as the young assistant hadn't been able to make her look life-like.

The medic appropriated the medical supplies and immediately injected a shivering Linda with a hefty dose of antibiotics as she asked, "You're not allergic to Penicillin, are you?"

Linda shook her head and promptly passed out.

Darren, in the meantime, sent several coolers of dry ice over to Mara's trailer to try and slow down the natural rotting process. He figured that three more good days ought to see the film finished. Then she could rot at will. He turned his attention back to Tony, who stood by the rest of the supplies.

"You got the collars?"

Tony grinned and held up a handful of heavy steel collars. "I know a couple of dominatrices who didn't mind lending their gear. What are we using them for?"

By the time Tony and another PA rounded up a dozen extras from the outside and locked them in one of the steel-sheeted storage units, the mortician had finished his makeup job on Mara. He beamed proudly as the actress was led out on a leash by one of the heftier grips.

"One of my better jobs, if I do say so myself," the mortician bragged. "Doesn't she look peaceful?"

She did indeed.

Darren rolled his eyes. "That's just great, but I don't *need* peaceful. She's supposed to be reacting to the death of her lover, not going for a drive in the country. Get my drift?"

The mortician sniffed. "I'll see what I can do."

"All right, people," Darren yelled. "Let's call it for the night. We'll pick this up tomorrow. Call time is six a.m.!"

A brief listen to the radio told Darren that things were not getting any better. The ratio of dead to living walking around in Los Angeles was rapidly favoring the dead. Citizens were advised to make their way to rescue shelters set up around the city. Darren felt the walled confines of Plateau Pictures were about as good a protection as anyone could ask for, and the other members of the production seemed to feel the same way – no one left the studio when he'd called it for the day.

It made Darren happy to be able to offer some safety to his cat and crew. He figured they deserved some compensation for the notoriously long hours that low budget productions demanded.

Tomorrow would be another sixteen-hour grind. Darren just hoped he'd be able to tell the live members of the production from the dead ones by the end of it.

The next day's shooting went relatively well although controlling the dead extras proved somewhat difficult. Several of the live extras were scratched and a production assistant bitten before all the ghouls had their mouths sewn shut. One of them ripped out the thread and managed to make a healthy lunch out of the makeup assistant. Phil took good look at her corpse and decided there was enough left to reanimate. "Someone put her in the extras pen."

Darren winced, but tried to look at it from the angle that it would save Tony from having to procure more bodies from the outside. He really didn't want to risk losing the kid to the extras en. Tony was the best P.A. Darren had ever worked with and he had that *spark*, the same sort of idealism that he, Darren, was rapidly losing. Darren wanted to see that spark -- not to mention Tony's health -- preserved.

All in all Darren was quite pleased with the acting jobs he was getting from his ghoulish thespians. They were easier to deal with than some of the crew, who were complaining about the smell. Wardrobe was especially vocal when it came to costuming the dead.

"Do you know how hard it is to get blood stains out of this material?" snapped the wardrobe girl who'd stitched Derrick's mouth shut. Darren hoped she'd become eligible for the extras pen. She wasn't that good of a seamstress either.

The medic, meanwhile, frantically tried to treat those who'd been bitten or scratched by the zombies, but the antibiotics didn't seem to be working.

On the upside, the dry ice was working well enough to prevent Mara and Derrick from degenerating too quickly. The hot lights were a bit of a problem, but that was what stand-ins were for.

Darren was coming to the reluctant conclusion that the zombie plague could be the best thing that had ever happened to his career.

At the end of the day Darren eagerly ran the dailies to see if they lived up to his expectations. Even Phil and Melissa were impressed with the improved quality of the stars' performances.

"Mara really looks horrified," Melissa commented during one scene.

"I think she was really hungry, " Phil said. "That was the scene we shot before lunch."

Darren felt a warm glow suffuse his entire being as the certainty that this, the end result, really was worth all of the … unpleasant things he'd had to do, the compromises he'd been forced to make. Sometimes true art could only be born out of the womb of horror.

Ignoring the pretentious tone of that last thought, Darren continued to watch the screen.

When they finished watching the dailies, Phil and Melissa headed off to get some supper while Darren rewound the film to view his masterpiece again in private. He'd only gotten through five minutes, however, when the door was opened and the light switched on.

Darren turned around in annoyance. "Didn't you see that the red light was on?" he snapped before his eyes adjusted to the light. He put a lid on his temper as soon as he registered who'd entered the room.

It was Gerald Fife, dressed as usual in relaxed-fit jeans and a silk shirt that did nothing to hide his middle-aged paunch or create the desired effect of borrowed youth.

"Gerald," Darren said expansively, confident that at last he had something of quality to show his executive producer. "Have a seat and check out these dailies."

"Sorry, ain't got time." Gerald sat down despite his words. "I'm just here to give you the news in person. Didn't want you to hear this through Phil." He pulled out a cigar and lit it.

Darren's heart plunged down into his stomach. "What news?" he asked, although he thought he knew the answer.

"I'm pulling the plug." Gerald took a long pull on his cigar, exhaling with obvious relish.

"What? Why?"

"This whole dead thing, Darren. It's depressing. The investors aren't going to want a movie about the Plague when the viewing public is already down about the zombies. No percentage in it."

"Jesus Christ, Gerald, you've got to take a look at these dailies!" Darren gestured toward the screen. "We've really got something now!"

Gerald shook his head with finality. "Sorry, Darren. No go. We're in this business to make money. No one's going to want to see a movie with a bunch of rotting bodies when they can look out their window and see the same thing for free."

"But—"

Gerald held up one hand, sending a plume of cigar smoke wafting in Darren's face. "But me no buts, kid, I ain't got the time. I wanna get out of here while I still can. Traffic's a bitch out there." He took a puff of his cigar." Sorry, kid. But you know what they say; when the going gets tough, the tough get going. And I'm getting the fuck out of Dodge." Gerald stood up. "Now where's Mara? I wanna give her the news myself."

Staring bleakly at the screen, Darren said, "She's locked in her trailer."

"Locked in?" Gerald's voice rose in outrage. "What the hell are you talking about, locked in?"

Darren started fumbling for an explanation. Suddenly his train of thought jumped to another track as something irrevocably snapped in his brain. He wasn't sure if it was his conscience or his sanity—maybe it was both—but it no longer mattered. Only the film mattered.

He stood up. "Sorry, Gerald. I meant she's locked *herself* in her trailer. Maybe you can help out."

"Jesus!" Gerald stubbed out his cigar. "What the hell did you do to her?"

"She's unhappy with the quality of the food we've had lately," Darren explained as he followed Gerald out of the screening room bungalow towards Mara's trailer. "It's been hard to get Cristal these days."

"On your budget it should be impossible, " Gerald snapped. "Damn good thing I'm shutting this down. The investors would have my balls for breakfast if they saw shit like that on the budget sheets. Jesus, what the hell is that smell?"

They were passing the warehouse housing the extras. Despite the heavy steel walls, the smell and the noise of the rotting extras gave the area a distinctly charnel atmosphere.

"Some meat gone bad," Darren said vaguely.

"What the hell are they doing in there?"

"Rehearsing one of the big crowd scenes."

"What a reek! How can anyone eat around here?" Gerald stepped up his pace. Darren matched it.

Mara's trailer sat before them, a steady unsatisfied moan emanating from inside.

"Jesus!" Gerald exclaimed. "She sounds like she's starving!"

Darren bounded up the steps before Gerald could see the industrial strength padlock on the trailer door. As he inserted the key, he tapped on the door and called, "Mara, Gerald's here to talk to you about a few things. You're going to have to unlock the door and let him in."

A rising moan answered him, along with the sound of Mara lurching through the trailer towards the sound of fresh meat.

"Let me up there, you asshole." Gerald pushed his way up the stairs just as Darren managed to remove the padlock. Slipping it into his pocket, he retreated to the ground and out of Gerald's way.

"Mara, baby, it's Gerald. Open the door, sweetheart! Uncle Gerald will take care of you."

Mara scrabbled at the door from the inside, moaning pitifully.

"Chris, she can't even talk!" Gerald said in horrified tones.

He grabbed the door handle and turned it. "Don't worry, baby, I'll feed you."

"I bet you will," Darren said cheerfully as Gerald opened the door. He watched as Mara grabbed hold of the executive producer's arms and pulled him inside. Darren helped with a well placed push on Gerald backside, then quickly slammed the door shut and replaced the padlock with a decisive snap.

"You know what they say," Darren called out as Gerald began screaming. "When the going gets tough, the tough get eaten!"

Darren smiled to himself. His first film, and it looked like he'd even get final cut.

--The End--

Death Bringer Jones

Thomas M. Malafarina

The lone figure walked silently through the underbrush doing his best not to make even the slightest of sounds. He knew a lot about them; about their kind. Unfortunately he didn't know everything and that concerned him. Yet this element of uncertainty added a degree of extra excitement to this hunt. He was, however was very much aware of their keenly enhanced senses. He knew they could see in the darkest night, smell even the faintest of scents and hear almost every sound no matter how distracted they might be.

That was why he had been careful to approach from downwind. He was the hunter and did not want to become the hunted. He knew there would be no way to completely mask his scent; his human smell. He only hoped the wind wouldn't shift. For if it did, his chances of walking out of the woods alive would be virtually non-existent.

As he got closer Death Bringer Jones, as he was known,

could hear the grunting and chewing sounds it made as the creature feasted on whatever or whomever it was currently devouring. Now that he was close he could see the victim, he noted it was a dismembered and disemboweled human corpse beneath the gory pile of bloody entrails steaming in the cold evening air. It must have been a recent kill, a really fresh one. And it appeared to be a young victim as well, perhaps a male in his early twenties; the chest flat and almost hairless.

Death Bringer suddenly realized half the reason he had made it this close to the beast was because the mutated thing was likely so preoccupied with its meal it had let its guard down. Otherwise, he was certain it would have sensed his approach. That's just how these creatures were made. The seldom missed such things.

The beast, this horrible freak of nature was huge, even in its squatted position. Its large block-like head sat practically down on top of its shoulders; its massive, muscular neck barely discernable. It had a large, overhanging fur-covered Neanderthal brow under which two beady black eyes darted back and forth, scanning the area always alert for trouble.

Those predatory eyes were sunk deep in dark-rimmed sockets bordered by high, strong cheekbones. Its nose was a huge flat thing reminiscent of a boxer's nose and had large flaring nostrils which seemed to be constantly sniffing the air. Its blood-covered dried and cracked lips were surrounded by a matted mass of facial hair, which did little to hide its hideous mouthful of shark-like teeth. These fangs were perfect tools for ripping and tearing living flesh.

It opened its huge tooth-filled maw and let go with a liquid-sounding belch of pure pleasure which echoed throughout the clearing. Even at more than ten feet away Death Bringer could smell the vile combination of foul breath, stomach contents and rancid blood drift by him. For a moment he worried he might not be able to hold back the impulse he felt, as his stomach was on the verge of vomiting. But he willed his insides to remain steady because he knew the sounds of his retching would surely give him away. Luckily, once the vile stench had passed by him, Jones took a few deep silent breaths and was once again able to regain control.

He bent down on one knee, took careful aim with his rifle getting the center of the mutant's massive block head directly in his sights. He knew the importance of this first shot; the kill shot. Because if it wasn't an instant kill, the thing might have enough life left in it to rip him to shreds before it finally died. He had seen such things happen to other hunters like himself. He let out his breath silently.

    Jones began to carefully apply pressure to the trigger then he heard something. The giant mutation apparently heard the sound as well because its huge head snapped surprisingly fast in the direction of the far side of the clearing. What Jones heard was a deep guttural groan coming from somewhere in the darkness. It was the sound those other creatures made; the undead ones.

    This brave new post-apocalyptic world of 2055 was crawling with bizarre creatures, one type as deadly as another. It was twelve years since the Zombie Virus of 2043 also known as the Z43 Virus had decimated the planet and almost wiped out the human race. Mankind had made a comeback, but the virus had mutated and now in addition to the living dead zombies a whole new host of freakish beings had begun to evolve; those monstrous mutants just being one of the new breed.

    And if Jones was right about what he suspected was

coming, he knew it would be best for him to wait for a few minutes and see how things played out. Just as this realization hit him Jones saw two of the wretched undead creatures lumbering clumsily out of the woods, arms outstretched; grunting, growling and moaning, heading straight toward the mutant creature and unknowingly to their own destruction.

Recognizing the approaching threat, the thing rose up from its crouched position effortlessly using the strength of its two massive muscular legs, which looked to Jones to be as big around as two tree trunks. Now the creature stood to its full height of close to eight feet of pure rippling leathery muscle. Jones ducked down in the underbrush not wanting to be seen by either the mutant or the two undead devils.

The mindless zombies paid no heed to the gargantuan-sized creature and continued shambling toward it. Then Jones realized they were not interested in the beast at all but in the same fresh pile of steaming flesh the creature was eating. Jones had heard rumors that sometimes these mutated mountains of muscle could walk freely among the undead without being attacked. He believed it might possibly have something to do with the scent the huge creatures gave off; some built-in aroma which fooled the zombies into believing they were one and the same. This scent, if it did exist apparently could only be released while the giants were alive. In fact, on more than one occasion Jones had actually seen clusters of the undead feasting on the corpses of these freakish monsters.

Regardless, two things immediately became very clear to Death Bringer Jones. The first had been that the two zombies wanted the pile of human remains. The second was that there was absolutely no way the massive beast was going to allow them to have it. Jones braced himself for the imminent confrontation which was about to take place.

As the first zombie approached the flesh pile and bent to feast the giant reached out one of its enormous clawed hands and grabbed the top of the undead creature's head. He squeezed tightly and Jones could hear crunching as its skull collapsed inward sending shards of bone fragments deep into its moldering decomposing brain. The zombie dropped to the ground in a heap, its head no more than squashed pulp like that of an orange trampled under the foot of an elephant.

The second undead creature showed absolutely no sign of

even noticing the destruction of its counterpart. Instead, it too reached for the tasty morsels of blood dripping intestines. The massive beast raised one of its muscular arms with its talon-like claws extended. With one incredible swipe, the creature separated the zombie's head from its shoulders and sent it flying over top of Jones's hiding place where it smashed against the side of a large tree. Jutting out from the tree, were a series of sharp, broken branches. One of those remnants pierced the back of the decapitated skull and shot out through the head's left eye socket. At the very tip of the pointy branch, which was slick with rotting gray matter, a single filmed eye dangled from slimy filaments. As Death Bringer Jones looked up at the horrific sight, a single drop of bloody vitreous fluid dripped down from the suspended eyeball and landed right in the middle of his forehead. Once again Jones was sure he was going to vomit but from behind him he heard the second zombie drop with a thud to the soft forest floor, reminding him of his own predicament and forcing him to once again remain in control.

    The behemoth dropped back to its squatting position and continued to dine on its feast as if it had never been interrupted.

For a few minutes, Jones's hands trembled from the effort of remaining quiet and desperately trying not to puke his guts out. Although he had dreamed of taking down one of these creatures for some time, now that he had seen exactly what they were capable of he worried he might not actually have what it took to kill one of these monsters.

Then he gave himself a mental pep talk, "You are Death Bringer Jones. You are legendary. You are a man without fear. You are killer of the undead, slayer of mutants and bringer of death to all creatures who dare to threaten you." After a few minutes of hiding and listening to the mutant slurping up the remainder of its kill Jones had sufficiently regained his composure and was ready to do what he had come here to do. He once again took position, aimed his rifle right between the beast's eyes then holding his breath he squeezed the trigger and the gun sounded with a deafening roar.

The thing's skull exploded out in all directions in a shower of brains, bone and gore. Most is its head had been annihilated leaving only the lower half of its jaw and a fragment of its chin. As Jones stared at the sight in amazement, the jaw seemed to momentarily move side to side just before the horrible headless corpse slowly tipped forward, falling into the bloody remains of its victims.

The sight was more than he could take. Jones took one last look around the clearing to make sure he was alone and then bent over with his hands on his trembling knees and began vomiting with more force than he would have believed possible. After a few moments which felt like a lifetime to Jones, his spasms subsided and he was once again able to stand up straight. Thank God that was over he thought.

Then he stood tall and took a deep breath. He had done it! He had slayed one of the biggest and deadliest of the mutant breed. He lifted his arms high, gun in hand in a celebratory gesture. But before he had time to truly appreciate his victory he felt a sharp stabbing pain in his lower back which shot right through to his stomach. He instinctively looked down and saw a huge clawed hand exploding out from his body with his intestines entangled in its hairy leathery fingers.

Death Bringer Jones had celebrated too soon. Death Bringer Jones had let his guard down. Death Bringer Jones had forgotten that he had not known everything about his prey. Death Bringer Jones had not considered that the creature he killed might have a mate or that this mate would be the bringer of his own death in this dark and lonely woods on this cold, cold night.

--The End--

Kitties and Zombies, Oh My!

Catt Dahman

A few weeks before, the man had been talking to himself and building courage. "Do it, really, and it's all fine. There's no pain," he said. He even looked down the barrel of the pistol as if resolution lay inside. He wanted to do it. He was talking himself into doing it, but he hesitated. He was still going over so many memories. He didn't pull the trigger.

A lot has changed since then.

He and one other person were walking, always quietly moving north. The stench was no better and no worse as they rounded a corner of a building, a library on a college campus, and found themselves in a tree shaded, brick-paved little park with benches and dried up flower beds. In fact, it was no better or worse than most of what they had seen for weeks, except for one change, a terrible addition to the usual horrors.

Amid the fallen leaves and along side the gnarled tree roots and the walkways were bits of fine fur, some of which stuck to the ground in ugly, bloody clumps and some of which floated on the slight breeze, only to collect on the far side of the park against a brown-and-maroon-streaked concrete wall.

Little broken and bitten bodies lay in the park but were neither eaten nor torn up. They were dead, but not in the common ripped apart, eviscerated, profane way that most dead humans ended up. There was a white corpse with a few drops of blood on its nose, a calico with her head twisted, and a grey-stripped tabby with a few cuts on his neck. There were ten times that many dead Zs.

    The little girl whooshed out a big breath of air and hid her face against the man's lower back for a few seconds as she trembled with fear and sadness. Over the past weeks, she had become almost immune to the *forever-dead* people that the *undead* had left behind. And there had been many *forever-dead* people, and because unlike television and movies, not only did a head injury kill these monsters, but so did extreme bodily damage and blood loss. If those who were bitten died before the virus took hold, they didn't get up and walk again.

"Kitties," the girl whispered, "just kitties."

"Yes, but those things got the worst of it. Look how many are lying around dead. Maybe we are close to a military unit or some group that's able to take out large hordes. That's a good thing," the man said.

"But kitties."

"I don't know."

Her little fists shook as she dared to look more closely at the carnage. "I thought the monsters only ate peoples, Jerum."

The man shrugged. His name was Jeremy, and the girl was six, bright, and capable of speaking quite well, but she had always called him *Jerum*, and he didn't bother to correct her.

For days after he found her, he tried to ignore her and hoped that she would go away and find other survivors to cling to, but she was like a stray cat herself, taking the bits of food he found for them, sharing his water, and curling up close.

After a few days, he let her walk beside him and began talking to her. She talked about ponies with long hair and girl singers with very short, colored hair and how she wished she knew how to braid her own hair. She chattered.

And when a horde with filthy nails came at them unexpectedly and trying to slice her tender face and feed on her, he pushed her behind him and fought their way free. That didn't mean he wanted a companion and certainly not one little and defenseless as she was, but he found himself unable to take the steps to rid himself of her.

So often while he was out scouting, he could have left her and never returned, but he always came back to her at their camp, and she never looked as if she doubted that he would return.

Sometimes he resented being burdened with a child, especially one he hadn't known before everything went so badly all over the world. Before the world became all about rot, teeth, claws, and moaning-hunger.

"Can we bury them?" she asked. She meant the cats.

Jeremy scowled a second. If he said no or didn't answer, she wouldn't cry or throw a fit. She wouldn't argue or plead, but only nod. But later, when it was cool and they lay next to a fire or in a corner wrapped in blankets or when it was dark and quiet, she would softly weep, so quietly that he knew she was trying to keep him from hearing.

He knew this because three times he had refused the burials: once when he found her hiding close to her dead parents and she wanted to bury them, once when she recognized a baby torn from a stroller and said it would only need a tiny grave, and once when she wanted to dig a hole for a sweet old woman who travelled with them a few miles before sitting down and drifting away into sleep and death.

It wasn't that he was heartless, but burials expended a lot of energy, and they found precious little water and food to replenish that. Besides, they were never safe enough in the open to take the time. They always had to be on the move.

But with a small shovel, he dug a hole in a flowerbed and scooped up the furry bodies, five in all, and then shoveled dirt on top of the grave. The girl gathered dead flowers, muttered a few words too quiet for Jeremy to hear, and gave him a nod.

"Jenny."

"What?"

"My name."

"Ah." Jeremy frowned. For weeks, she had allowed him to call her *Girl*, refusing to tell him her name when she was most afraid or during the rare moments of peace and security they shared or when she talked about her family. He understood now that refusing to tell him her name was her childish act of defiance for not allowing proper burials. He was amused but kept his face neutral.

On the days that he tried to tease her name from her, he had gotten angry at her rebelliousness and spent time rebuking her. It had been far better for his mental state than if he had spent the time looking at all the dead and thinking about how hopeless their situation was.

She lowered her head, but tears filled her lashes and ran down her dirty cheeks; she was ashamed and regretful. "It's easier to bury a li'l ole stray, Jerum, than a friend with a name. I have…had a kitty, too. His name was Foxxy. I'd be so sad to have to bury him, but…but…oh, Jerum, maybe he never got buried at all." She suddenly wailed and ran for him.

Jeremy let the shovel fall and grabbed her into his arms and held her as she sobbed. Her tense body shuddered with pain. As he stroked her long golden hair, he fought against a memory of his own, of soothing a child that smelled of lavender and who had long, pretty hair. A scraped knee. A sad movie. A bad dream. His throat ached so badly that it felt as if knives were being thrust into his neck, and his only salvation from the pain was to open his mouth and let out his braying cries, howls from deep within his chest.

After a while, both stopped crying and parted, a weight lifted from each.

"Did you lose a kitten, too?"

Jeremy fought back fresh tears. "Yes, I guess you could say that."

"What was its name?"

"Elizabeth."

Jenny gave him a quick nod and a pat on the hand as she picked up the shovel for him. Caring the shovel and leading him by his hand, she crept back to the library where she waited for him to listen and sniff and decide if this might be a place to rest for the night. There were a few signs that a battle had been waged inside: the door and windows were broken, but back among some of the shelves was an alcove where they could sleep.

He showed her how he would block it off, and if anything came close, she *must* climb up high and get away. He'd be close behind.

By a dim flashlight, he checked his pistol and set his knife at the ready before digging out a meager meal from his pack: crackers, a box of raisins, a few sticks of beef jerky, and a can of soda that he had been holding back. Seeing Jenny smile, as wan as it was, and seeing a little pleasure in her eyes as she savored her half of the soda made Jeremy both sad and a little happy.

"Why were the kitties here?"

"I don't know." It was what he answered to almost all of her questions. Why had the undead returned to bite and spread a virus? *He didn't know.* Was help coming? *He didn't know.* Would things get better? *He didn't know.*

He was just a man who, some how had been at

home, a place where he was able to stay away from the monsters, to pack a backpack, and to bring along his gun; that was all that saved him. His family, out getting pizza, had not been lucky. And no, he hadn't had the mental strength to bury them either. He had burned the building instead.

He had been ready to put a bullet into his own head when he heard the girl, Jenny, moving to a new position and had caught a glimpse of her blue dress, sky blue, the same color his own *kitten* had been wearing when the monsters came and took her and her mother away from him.

Before they slept, Jeremy checked outside and listened and watched. The moon was bright and the sky cloudless, and he saw tiny orbs set in sets of two reflecting the moonlight. Little eyes. He didn't understand the oddity, but he didn't feel threatened, so he went back and fell asleep, probably sleeping the deepest he had in the last few weeks.

Neither he nor Jenny had nightmares.

When he awoke, something gnawed at his brain like an itch, and he had to solve a riddle before it drove him mad.

"Stay here," Jeremy pointed to a bench.

As Jenny watched, Jeremy walked over to the dead humans, to the creatures who were truly dead. Before, he had assumed that a roaming military group or a group of survivors had shot them because many times they found those types of scenes, leftover events that Jeremy and Jenny missed. They were never able to catch up to the larger group of well-armed people that the pair envisioned.

Jeremy didn't like looking at the mottled, rotting flesh and had to breathe through his mouth in shallow gulps as he leaned closer to the bodies, but he was right in that none had been torn apart to the extent needed to kill them. He used a stick to move their heads about to check. None of the bodies had broken necks. None had bullet or knife wounds to their heads. Subconsciously, he noticed this the evening before. But it was twilight, and he was too tired to think about the strangeness.

He moved away and again might have missed the obvious, except as he turned, he looked down to avoid stepping on a woman's greenish-grey leg and saw something peculiar. Quite clearly was a small bite wound with no more than a nickel-sized patch of flesh removed. A dried bit of skin lay an inch away from her leg as if the tiny bit of flesh had been spat away. Black streaks ran up and down her leg like blood poisoning.

With fresh eyes, he looked at another corpse and saw a nasty, deep bite on its arm. No flesh was torn away, but the teeth prints were black against the skin, and the streaks were evident. A third had a bite on her ankle. And another had a bite on her neck with livid scratches along her arms as if she had tangled with briars.

Or claws.

Jeremy sat on the bench beside Jenny and pondered this.

"I think the kitties got them," Jenny said.

Jeremy swallowed hard and nodded slowly. "Maybe." What this meant, he didn't know. The animals had always been safe, but now, he was unsure about that. He eyed a black bird that pecked at a man's face.

They walked across the campus expecting to be attacked, but the day was quiet, and there were none of the usual moans that would have turned their spines ice cold. The stillness made Jeremy nervous.

As they turned the corner at the science building, Jeremy pushed Jenny back against the wall and held a finger to his lips, but as he looked at the tableaux, he saw corpses as well as a few cats and kittens washing their paws and sunning themselves. One cat, a big grey and white fellow, had a green collar and little bell around his neck. He blinked at Jeremy.

Jeremy went back the way they came to scout for another route. While nothing seemed ominous, he didn't feel it was wise to backtrack. When he turned, Jenny was not against the wall where he left her.

For the first time in weeks, something more than fear overwhelmed Jeremy; it was primordial terror, rage, and sorrow. His heart hammered as he ran and skidded around the corner.

Jenny sat on the sidewalk petting the grey and white tomcat and cooing to it. The cat's muzzle, once pristine white, was slightly pink. Jeremy shivered.

"Get away from him. Move slowly." He kept his gun on the cat and walked sideways, trying to get closer.

"Jerum, no, no! Don't you dare hurt him," Jenny had never raised her voice and had never argued, but her face was a mask of anger.

"He. I think. Jenny, do what I said."

"They bited the monsters and killed them. You said it," her voice became singsong. "You said that we needed a miracle because the monsters had won and we were doomed."

He had said that, but not *to her*. To himself as he ran the end of the pistol over his temple and then his jaw, trying to decide where to shoot himself as he sat alone. He said it right before he found *her* skulking about. He had been talking aloud and readying himself to die. He narrowed his eyes thinking she was tricking him and being deceptive.

"So you think cats are attacking the Zs and that the bite kills them like *their* bite kills us…or makes us undead?"

Jenny shrugged. "It isn't much sillier to think about that, is it?"

He felt faintly like the butt of a joke that he didn't understand. "It's just…."

He saw the human corpses and the satisfied faces of the cats. Small, younger cats scampered into the bushes to play. One very small kitten, maybe just weaned if that, was curled in Jenny's lap purring contentedly. Jenny had a point. It really was no harder to believe *that* than anything else he had seen for weeks.

"I think they'll follow us. They can help. Can they

come with us, Jerum?"

"I doubt we could stop them," he said honestly. A faint bloom of hope took root in his heart, but he also felt a distant, bittersweet moment as he realized that maybe his role and her role had altered slightly.

She rose and brought the kitten in her arms, carrying it like a baby doll. Her thumb in her mouth. Her arms were full, but she leaned against his side and hugged Jeremy as best she could. "Mommies and Daddies still take care of the kittens."

"Is that so?" He hugged her close. The big tom walked close and kept watch over the kitten Jenny held.

Jenny's giggle was something Jeremy had never heard, but it was joyous and pure. "Silly kitties. They are getting their new teeth." She held out the thumb she was sucking, and two tiny pricks of blood dotted her skin. The kitten had been teething on her thumb, as baby animals will do sometimes.

What was in their saliva that made their bites lethal to the undead? Did they get the virus in their mouths and spread it? Sudden fear washed Jeremy again, and his legs felt so weak that he slid down to sit on the warm sidewalk. The tom came over and used his head to rub against Jeremy's arms and side.

"I hope you can save us. I really do. And I believe you can. But…." Jeremy glanced again at the tiny specks of blood on Jenny's thumb. "But if you mess with my *kitten*, I'll make you sorry."

Three Zs moved into view, and a pair of ginger cats ran over and nipped at their ankles; the monsters fell within a few seconds and didn't move again. Jeremy found it fascinating, but he was still leery.

Jenny clapped. "It's okay, Jerum. Don't you see, now?"

"See?"

"Now, the kittens are in charge. They're gonna rule the world. Isn't that wonderful? A world of kitties."

Jeremy relaxed. Maybe she was right. Cats were inheriting the world. He sneezed and made a mental note to begin looting all the allergy medicines he could find.

"Hold the baby. He likes to chew and nip, but it doesn't hurt much at all. Do it, really, and it's all fine. There's no pain," said Jenny as she shuffled the kitten into his arms.

"No pain," Jeremy said as he held the kitten close and hugged Jenny closer.

It was *only* about being with the kittens. *His* kitten.

--The End--

Pleasure Island

Wesley Thomas

Trevor loved theme parks, ever since childhood. The roller coasters, gift shops, food, and energetic atmosphere thriving in the bustle of energetic people. But Pleasure Island was more than just a place of enjoyment to Trevor, it bore a greater significance than frivolous fun.

Pleasure Island was where his parents went missing when he was only seven years of age. Whilst on a ride catered for the younger crowd, with his parents watching, full of pride. Trevor spun and spun, smiling and giggling until the ride came to an end. He wobbled from the ride and looked to the crowd of parents, to find his had vanished. He began shouting their names, then crying, but was ultimately taken away by the authorities. After a long battle, and the parents nowhere to be found, it was decided his aunt and uncle would be the legal guardians.

Any sane person would avoid the park like a stalker, yet Trevor actually found happiness in his annual visits. As it was the last place he saw his parents. He could still visualize them taking him for candy floss, queuing for rides or swimming in one of the many pools. Trevor, now eighteen, made sure every year, around October, he could visit Pleasure Island. This year the theme park was holding a special event in celebration of Halloween. Visitors could explore the park in the early hours and even go on the rides in the cover of darkness. Trevor, having a fondness for horror movies, books and generally all things spooky, jumped at the opportunity. So one evening whilst browsing the net in his cramped bedroom, he booked one ticket for 'Spooktacular Scares at Pleasure Island'.

A week later, at 1am on October 31st no less, Trevor used a bar code from his smart phone to gain entry to the park. The weather was chilly, so fortunately he had attired in a dark, thick hoody with jeans and comfy skaters shoes hugging his feet. But the second he entered the park the air seemed to become even colder, giving Trevor a delightful chill. But he was so excited that he paid no attention to the decline in warmth. He was more interested in hopping on rides and slinking around in the gloom. The park was pretty quiet. A few people were scattered around, some queuing for rides, others waiting outside restrooms, and some teenagers fooling around. It was difficult to make much out as the only lights were jack-o-lanterns and other Halloween themed lighting fixtures draped throughout the park. Illuminated skeleton heads were nestled into darkened corners, glowing corpses were tossed onto haystacks, and evil, yellow eyes swarmed the woods just beyond the park, outside the tall sturdy fences. The thought of so many eyes carousing Trevor made him tingle. Spookiness at its greatest, which gave Trevor reason to smile as he strolled along, soaking up the scenery and observing fellow visitors in their pursuit of terror. There was no particular route in mind, he was absent-mindedly wandering along when he came to the children's ride where his parents had vanished all those years ago. Or technically, the new ride which had replaced it.

This stung him. He stopped and fought for breath as that ride meant something to him. Pleasure Island was clearly more interested in getting rid of kiddy rides and bringing in adult rides to attract more tourists and, of course, money. A tear escaped Trevor's eye, trailing his rosy cheek as he scrunched his lips feeling mournful, stifling sobs. That silly little ride was a way, the only way, to remember clearly what his parents looked like, besides photographs. However, things change, he knew that. So he shrugged off his mournful attitude and embraced the new ride, giving it a gander. Crimson metal poles with a few people queuing inside red painted wood, with a huge sign above reading 'Coaster to Hell' in gigantic red font that looked as if it was oozing blood. A loud giggle from behind startled Trevor as a small group of teens brushed by him and joined the queue. He wanted to see what the fuss was about, and see if this new coaster was worth replacing the children's ride. But something rubbed him the wrong way about the coaster to hell. A strange, unidentifiable aura emanated from the ride, giving Trevor goosebumps. Which was strange given his passion for all things horror, but this feeling was different. It was beyond anticipation and slight nerves, this was a bright beacon flashing relentlessly into his subconscious, blaring loud. Was it warning him? He couldn't distinguish this new found awareness. Either way, it wasn't going to stop him strolling to the herd of people. His hand smoothed along the metal poles as he crept towards the queues. It felt cold and the paint smelled fresh. Given that this wasn't anything unusual as it was a new ride. People had seemingly sprung from nowhere. At first only a short collection were within the poles. But now the gathering had thrived and spawned around thirty people. From what Trevor could see, they were all youngsters, around his age if not younger. Which was not surprising given most adults would bring their very young children at a more reasonable hour than 1am. Also, scariness wasn't exactly appropriate for infants. Trevor was looking forward to a quiet, creepy tour by himself. *I guess not anymore.* He tutted as the line shrunk and he scuttled closer to the darkness that was swallowing the guests one by one.

    Trevor came to the dark space, behind an individual gate that told him he was next to sit in the coaster tram. People fell in their seats and eagerly yanked their harnesses overhead, safely securing them in place for sensible thrills. Trevor was still itching from an unknown anxiousness as to the possibility of something much more insidious than a ride lurking in the dusk. Ride attendants jogged by each person, checking the harnesses, some advising riders to hand their loose objects to them for safe-keeping until the ride came to an end. The man collecting personal belongings was undeniably creepy, with shadowy eyes and pale skin, with a bald head that shined in the murk. He slinked along grinning as he took hats, sandals, jewelry, cameras and phones. Soon enough they were off; the rattling of the chain echoed amongst the cheers of eager thrill-seekers. One by one the ride vanished into darkness, their whoops also fading. The gate before Trevor then unlocked and creaked open, allowing him to sneak forwards and prepare to mount the next tram. With no one behind, it looked like Trevor would be riding alone. As he waited patiently, Trevor admired the freakish decor. Flashing signs telling people to leave to instill cowardice, red licks of paint giving the impression of blood splatters, more Halloween decorations hanging like bodies from nooses, and advisory health signs. Anyone pregnant, suffering from heart conditions or vertigo was to leave now.

"I heard that Vicky from school rode this ride and was never seen again," some girl from behind gossiped amongst her friends, which caught the attention of Trevor.
"Shut up! No she didn't, that is such a pile of crap, you're just trying to scare us," another girl replied laughing.
"No I swear, honestly, have you seen Vicky? Think about it. She loved horror so came to the midnight opening event of this ride. No one has seen her since," the storyteller whispered.

There was an unsettling pause that spread through the crowd of voices. Trevor turned sideways in an attempt to view the chatter boxes. But all that could be made out were eyes and teeth in the dimness.

"Wait, you talking about that manic depressive chick who always skips class?" a guy butted into the conversation from another group, bluntly.

"Well yeah, but she came to school at least a few times a week, but she has been gone for weeks, there are missing signs everywhere. Haven't you seen 'em?" she asked.

"That chick is probably doing it for attention or something," he scoffed.

A screeching pulled Trevor's focus from the chitchat to the oncoming tram. Which was empty. Before becoming irrational he told himself that hundreds of coasters now had more than one actual coaster as to get the line moving faster. The conversation soon died down, and within seconds was replaced with more energetic whoops and roars of excitement.

"Please take your seat ladies and gentlemen, for your ride to hell!" the speaker system reverberated into the sombre.

Trevor carefully stepped into the cart, falling into the embrace of warm, wet leather seats. He slumped inside and pulled over the safety harness until it clicked into place. Butterflies fluttered in his stomach as his head became hot. People jumped into the carts to his front and back, slamming down safety belts, laughing and joking. He often envied people who could smile through life, having no worries, completely satisfied with their existence. Trevor suffered from the occasional depression and anxiety, often finding it difficult to project a smile when he wasn't genuinely happy, which unfortunately, wasn't very often. The only time he was truly happy was at home reading a chilling tale or watching a horror flick. Being in a crowd of people made him uncomfortable. Even one-on-one with a close friend sometimes created anxiousness. Yet again the attendants came round checking the harnesses were firmly in place. Followed by the creepy bald dude taking even more items. Trevor noticed he scuttled with a hunch, like some creepy goblin. He had a nervous energy about him, and the ongoing creepy aura, which made Trevor on edge when the creeper came to his tram.

"Any loose items?" he breathed, a rancid odor blowing into Trevor's face. An unnaturally vile stench.

"No, thanks," Trevor responded, eager for him to slither along.

What was that smell? His breath was hellish! He grumbled to himself.

The man holding a bag of valuables disappeared into blackness, sniggering. *Relax, maybe his behavior was all part of the show? To go that extra mile to unnerve people.* Just as the roller coaster chugged to life, taking off. "Please stay seated, assholes and elbows on the seats at all times," the speaker advised, receiving claps and chortles from the more rambunctious riders.

Trevor's grip tightened on metal hand rails attached to the black leather harness. *This is it.*

The coaster started, pulley system rattling into the void they were being pulled into. The enthusiastic screams and shrieks only heightened, which made Trevor more apprehensive. He could tell they were being taken up, although visually all he could see was a bright light hovering in the distance. Trevor let his head sink back in preparation for what would no doubt be a rocket speed launch. Every roller coaster was in competition for the faster ride with the largest g-force, pushing the boundaries of safety. So he figured, best to be safe rather than sorry. Head-banging was fine at Gothic clubs and metal music gigs, but not on a rollercoaster. The ride soon came to a halt, and a countdown began by a robotic voice echoing into the dimness. The light that Trevor had seen minutes ago was a black electronic board that was now showing numbers in a countdown from ten. Every rider, save for Trevor, joined in the countdown, bellowing into the blackness, added with howls from immature young men. Trevor's pulse increased as the countdown was nearing its completion. 3. He gulped. 2. He took a deep breath. 1. His face creased as air whipped into it with mighty force. Trevor could feel his skin become taut and attire whipping wildly. The ruckus of wheels on tracks ricocheted from walls, as did everyone's shouting. Trevor was pleasantly surprised; the ride was enjoyable, and his heart rate eased. A smile even found its way onto his face, dimples forming tiny dents in his cheeks. Not that he or anyone else could see them. His stomach performed somersaults as the tracks began to loop, swirling and spinning, sending his dark hair into a frenzy. Trevor released a laugh. It was the first time he had laughed in a very long time. Maybe this was just what he needed. His anxiety and depression had fled his mind; he was in the moment, enjoying life, as every older person often advised. That was until the ride came to a screeching halt, which felt premature. It wasn't over, they weren't back at the queue with eager people in the line waiting to hop onto the coaster; they were still in lightlessness.

"Hey, what gives?" a boy moaned, which everyone responded too with a collaboration of mutual boos and complaints, mixed in with crass language and crude remarks.

Trevor's short lived joy had been replaced by distress, his skin twitching in anticipation of the unknown. *Had the coaster broke down?* Then something huge hit Trevor's cart. He screamed, expecting a bunch of laughter at his outburst, but even more shrieks dominoed through the abyss. He couldn't see a damn thing, but could hear an orchestra of screeches. From manly bellows to womanly yells. Which is when the ride started up again, yet something felt different. The cries of fellow riders faded, and the dark became malignant. Trevor felt eyes watching him as the coaster delicately skidded along. Irrationally his head lashed back and forth, eyes darting into the gloom, searching for light. Perhaps a glowing exit sign or Halloween decoration. But it was pitch-black. *What the fuck is going on?* Trevor lost his breath after abruptly turning in his seat. His individual two-seater was apparently detached from the roller coaster and was deviating from the tracks. "Help!" He gave in, wailing hysterically. But nobody responded. "Please, anybody? Hello?" he continued, beckoning for assistance. There was nothing, he was alone. Until he heard somebody eerily giggle. And this giggle didn't sound in the least bit friendly. A wave of heat bloomed in Trevor as he squeezed onto the metal hand grips, praying that it was just his imagination, or part of the ride. But there it was again. A high-pitched chuckle slithering in the abyss. He took deep breaths silently, eyes flickering around, even though there was still no light. But illumination wasn't needed to identify his cart smashing into something again.

Trevor jerked, word-vomit causing him to scream, which received more insidious laughter. But something more frightening followed the sinister amusement: a ripe stench that hit Trevor like a punch to the face. He fought back vomit as the repugnance wafted into his face. It was akin to the reek of death. Blood, mold, rot, and an unidentifiable rankness. That was it, Trevor wanted off this ride and out of here. For the first time in his life, he no longer wanted to be in Pleasure Island.

As he spasmed in his seat, fighting against the harness, Trevor realized he was trapped. He was helpless but to go wherever the tram took him. The aroma only intensified as the ride strolled along an uneven track, sending painful vibrations through the seats. Perspiration leaked from his head and seeped into his eyes, stinging them. Trevor reached to rub away the sweat but his arms were held back by the safety restraints. So he squeezed his eyes shut and then blinked relentlessly, trying to eradicate the itchy burning. In the midst of his struggle, through blurred vision, a dim light broke through the dusk. This made Trevor pause, distracting him from his eyes, which were beginning to feel better as his focus was averted to the carnage that encompassed him. The ride was moving through the ultimate house of butchery. Bodies strewn across a graveled ground, dismembered, severed and bloody. Trevor wanted to believe these were just very realistic props, all part of the experience, beating out competitors. But denial wasn't an option given the vile stink permeating into his pores, and smearing onto his tongue. Terrified, Trevor continued bashing against the leather coated belt. He knew it was useless, but it was all he could do to not throw up. The air was completely polluted with the rankness, poisoning oxygen to the point where Trevor wished he was a vampire and didn't have to breathe. Also, the ongoing ride didn't help his sickness. Being stood and overlooking the manslaughter was bad enough, moving in a roller coaster tram in solitude, only with a dim light giving subtle illumination, made it significantly worse. *The light!* He never identified the actual light source. Trevor crossed his fingers in hope that it was an emergency exit. Not that it would do him any good as he was-

    The electronically activated harness abruptly flipped up after a click and ding. It flung overhead, allowing freedom. They clanged loudly, met with more chuckling. Trevor, not wanting to find out who or what was laughing like some deranged psychopath, fumbled with the small belt at his waist and unbuckled it, freeing himself. He vaulted from the ride, dripping in sweat, heart racing and lungs aching. The light was a small bulb swinging above, now with an eerie creak. *Had it always been swaying? Or had someone pushed it?* Then something tickled Trevor's neck.

He shrieked, crawling over the ride as it persevered through bloody bodies. Trevor scrambled over the leather seats, holding the railings and jumping off the other side and racing into the blackness. Trevor was horrified. Bones crunched underfoot, body organs were squeezing, some exploding and splashing onto Trevor's jeans. The mountain of bodies grew, as he realized he was literally climbing through corpses.

With the subtle light still moving back and forth, the giggling amplifying and the pile of dead folk thickening, Trevor was fearful of how it could get any worse. Which was when he fell, landing in the mess of victims. Limbs everywhere, blood slippery, and jelly-like guts and intestines squelching under his writhing petrified body. Cold flesh appeared to be everywhere, dipped in various body fluids, stinking beyond belief. Trevor crawled frantically, wriggling through the dead. When a pile of wallets and purses came into sight. Rucksacks, phones, jewelry, keys, and wallets were in a separate assortment near the bloody chopped up people. But it was one particular wallet, nestled into the bottom, that stood out. It was a blue, green and purple wallet, with a photo of an old rock band printed onto the worn and shredded cotton. Trevor waded through the mass of appendages and yanked it from the stash of belongings. A few wallets tumbled in the process, rolling amongst veins, eyeballs and peeled off flesh. He trembled opening the wallet, relying on the dim light washing the area in light every two seconds, still dangling overhead. Then Trevor saw it: a photo of his parents inside. This was his father's wallet. A tear escaped his eye as his lips began to wobble. They were somewhere amongst the bloodshed. As he gently sobbed, the light above was switched off. Which made the group of cackles all the more clear. Not just one, but a bunch of laughter surrounding him.

"Supper time boys," a southern accent hissed through the blackness, followed by tones of cackles.

Figuring he may as well try to prevail this nightmare, he held the wallet tight and stumbled through the disarray. The ruckus of crunching and squishing sounded from everywhere as he barged through the graveyard of bodies, attempting not to trip on cartilage or slip on blood. There had to be a way out, after all the coaster came in through a door. *The coaster!* Trevor could still hear it jutting along in the despair. He followed the sound, changing course, hoping it would lead him from this decaying hell hole. Uneven ground transformed into a smoother surface with tiny hard boards running horizontally across the floor. *The tracks!* Running was now far easier, as the noise the coaster produced became louder. Trevor was nearing it. The snickering and eager panting were fading, as the chattering of the wheels on tracks sounded so close. Until Trevor tripped and flopped into the sweaty leather seat, banging his head and eventually slumping onto the floor of the cart.

Feeling more optimistic he brought his legs in and snuck under the seats, hiding from plain sight. But in total darkness he questioned how these creatures were able to run so uninhibited. It hadn't appeared that they repeatedly fell or crashed into objects. *How could they see?* The cart then bashed into something, but continued on. *Another set of doors? The way out? Have I escaped?* Trevor allowed a smile to wriggle onto his face and hope to glow in his heart. He cautiously crept from under the seats and stood on the moving coaster, which abruptly came to a halt. Not expecting this Trevor flipped over the seats in a blur of subtle blackness. He landed hard on what felt like concrete. Cold, sharp and crumbly. Trevor's mind whirling he began to stand, actually able to see in this room due to multiple bulbs suspended from black cables. These several lights exposed what looked like an underground cave. An abundance of shadows, hundreds more carcasses sprawled on the rock, blood splatters, insides on the outside, and a small lake. In the middle of the cave, several meters down, was a little pool of water. Bodies were floating at the surface, red mists circling each one, and a dark crimson tainted the lake's floor. It was a lake of more corpses. As

Trevor toyed with the idea of vomiting, debating if it would make him feel better, someone breathed into his ear.

A hot rancid breath that compelled the hairs on his neck to stand on edge. "There's nowhere to run," someone spat, speckles of saliva spraying Trevor.

Just as Trevor was considering his next move the thing bulldozed him down into the water. Trevor spun, vision a blur of rock, blood and flesh. In the descent he could make out a pack of the monsters through his blurred spinning vision. There was at least fifty of them stood watching him plunge into the bloody bath of the dead. It was as he splashed into the filthy water, landing on a body and falling underwater, that something hit him. He couldn't escape this. One or two maybe he could fight through, but fifty, no way. On the bright side, he would likely die near where his parents did. That was his last thought as the horde of cannibals surged into the water and began chomping into him. Flesh was ripped off, organs devoured, and muscle savagely consumed by ravenous flesh-eaters. Until the only thing that was left, was Trevor's fear-stricken face.

Regret

Amanda M. Lyons

Their stench rose in waves of must and age, of rot and mildew, like dark death himself, sweet and repellent. They marched in a terrible wall of destruction, hungry for the flesh of our people, their living counterparts, they tore through the streets of New Castle and consumed everything.

In the New Castle Church of Christ the recently deceased Timothy Bondman climbed out of his casket and bit into Reverend Miller's outstretched hand. The beloved Reverend shrieked in blood curdling horror as Timmy pressed him to the floor and continued to devour him, rending flesh from muscle with knotted fists and tearing teeth. The mourners ran from their pews, pushing and shoving to get to the doors, trampling a few of their "brethren" beneath their crushing feet, throwing the doors wide only to be swallowed up by the wall of death, rushing headlong into the very end they'd been running from. The dead walked among us and we fell rendered at their feet.

    I drive away in utter horror and yet I find myself absorbed in the gory and seemingly endless death caught in my rearview mirror. I can't help but wonder how it feels to be torn apart, a rag-doll caught between struggling monsters. The dead follow. They're close enough that a victim's blood spatters onto my back window; I can only shudder as the unfortunate Joey Warner, a teenage paperboy, is devoured alive. When his corpse falls it lands first on my trunk and then catches on my rear bumper. I step on the gas, trying to put distance between me and them, the terrible thud of his body striking pavement and dragging behind me a revolting reminder of all that I have left behind. I know that this is the end of everything and it is all my fault.

    My name is Abigail Brennan, I am, or rather was, an author of S/M novels. I'd never really liked what I was writing, it was such a strange topic for me, I didn't do these things in my life. I had never acted on these images, though they tantalized me in secret. In self-disgust and desperation I tried to move over to the dark and macabre world of horror, something safer and less personal. My interests took me in another direction however, where the darkness was real and promised more tangible possibilities. The occult offered me new direction and the potential for a new level of being. I took this feeling and I ran with it, I ran until I found something that I couldn't ignore, a way to feel as I had when I'd first begun to write, that feeling I had lost as I grew to hate what I was as an author. It consumed me, a spell that would come to change everything, a spell to rend the world.

I didn't know that then. I only saw it for what it promised me, the gift of being the world's best storyteller, a Scheherazade of phenomenal status, more than the hack I had been and it seemed I would always be.

One dark night I set out to perform the ritual it required. The greatest mistake I have ever made. I wasn't thinking, consumed by greed, the desire to be more than I was. I would beg God for forgiveness, but I have never believed there is or ever was such a being. That night I murdered four men. Just how I managed to evade being caught I have no idea. I made so many mistakes in killing those men, it all seemed so obvious. Perhaps darker forces were at work.

I got out of bed as silently as I could, leaving my lover

asleep in our bed as I crept to the door and out of his apartment. The night was as dark as it can be in New York, with only streetlights and window light to combat the shadows on the street.

I'd planned it all out beforehand; I wanted to get it all done without being spotted. I'd scanned the streets for weeks before I was certain I had the right source for the hearts required for the ritual. You see, even my stay with Robert had been planned. The alley beside his apartment building was a frequent home for the men I intended to murder.

As I approached the alley tingles of electricity started to move up and down my body, the danger of the moment was finally getting to me, making my nerves jangle and the hair on my body stand on end. I was terrified and exhilarated at the same time, anticipating the act as much as what it would bring me. I pushed aside any thoughts of abandoning it, justified by the knowledge that it could bring my life some new sense of purpose, but terrified I was going mad. I managed to pull the knife from my boot without cutting myself, taking a breath to prepare and try to soothe my nerves.

I walked into the alley and found them where I had

expected, sleeping their inebriated sleep spread-eagle on the ground or leaning against a wall. There were four, four hearts was what I needed. The street was quiet, Robert didn't live in a bad neighborhood, but the crime here was still high enough to warrant empty streets after midnight, I would have both time and security if I didn't draw attention to myself.

    I grabbed the first by an arm and drug him into the next alley so that I wouldn't disturb the others. I needed four and I wanted to get them as quickly as possible. The first, second, and third were easy, they'd been sedated by the liquor, hardly disturbed by my moving them. They only reacted when it was already too late, their blood running out as I cut their hearts from their bodies and slid them into the deep pockets of my overcoat.

    When I came back for the fourth he stood guzzling from a bottle. His steps staggered, he walked toward me, his bleary eyes on mine were confused and half-lidded. The sight of him sent a shock of fear through me. What if I was about to be caught?

    "Where's my friends?"

    I didn't say anything. Reacting without much thought, I closed the space between us and, tracing a finger over his chest, I tried to put on my most charming leer. "Oh, they're over there, but I think we might have a little business of our own." I cooed it, trying not to breathe in the smell of alcohol on his breath.

"Yeah, maybe." He slurred with a new light of lust in his rheumy eyes. He ran his hand over my cheek, to my neck, and before he could go lower I pulled him into a kiss, locking our lips together before I drew my knife. I maneuvered him against the closest wall and pressed him there, keeping our mouths together as I stabbed him. I swallowed his scream and let him fall to the ground as I pulled the blade out of the wound. I'd hit him just below the voice box, severing his vocal chords so there wouldn't be any sound.

A terrible wheezing sound came from him as I worked, taking the last heart as quickly as I could and fleeing the scene. Covered in blood as I was, I felt invisible, the black of my clothes hid most of it from sight, there was no one to see it as I moved, panting as I rushed down the street and around another corner toward the old fur warehouse where I'd left my other supplies.

I walked into pale candlelight, the tacky blood on my skin popped into vision as the light grew. I'd lit the candles a few hours before, wanting to be ready when I'd finished. I combined the Dragon's Blood, Bergamot, and sulphur with the hearts and a parchment with the incantation written on it in an urn. When they were combined I lifted the urn over my head and invoked the names the spell had listed for each of the directions, my circle shuddering with the pull of energy I drew in, calling their names. I felt a charge go through my body as I worked, and a pounding as the hearts began to beat in their container. So far the spell had gone as intended.

    I set the urn down on the ground, careful not to disturb whatever forces made them beat as I moved. The hearts began to pulse faster and faster until they caught flame and were burned into dust. My offering had been accepted. The candles around me flared into full flame, their wax pouring from the wick as I walked out of the building and away from the roaring blaze. I'd only walked a few feet before it was engulfed, the explosion throwing my hair up around me as I moved, the greasy air blowing past me with shards of glass and metal. I was untouched, a maniacal laughter coming from me as I walked back toward Robert's street. I got inside and had a shower before he'd even stirred.

When I awoke in the morning I kissed Robert and headed out onto the street. There were two cruisers parker near the alley. I worried for a moment and then I saw the apathy with which they handled the scene, two of the officers were handling the bodies loosely and with little formality while two more leaned against the cruiser drinking coffee and eating donuts as if nothing were wrong. I walked around the block and then around a corner into an alley where I doubled over with laughter, my nerves had overtaken me, swallowing me with nervous laughter.

After a few minutes, I continued toward home.

When I sat down in front of my computer I had expected to be able to write, but when I turned the computer on I couldn't think of a single word. The enormity of what I'd done echoing in my skull. In a rage, I got up and threw the monitor across the room. The pictures and my college diploma shook in their frames and fell to the floor below. I tore around the room, grunting and screaming, yanking things from walls and tearing my desk apart, wrenching apart the spines of several of my published novels. I had killed for nothing! Nothing! The printer sat accusingly on a table next to where the desk had been and I threw it. The machine on which I had printed many senseless and stupid books slammed into the opposite wall.

I heard a dark and humorless laugh erupt from somewhere in the room. I looked around, my mind moving like a finger through pudding, and I realized it was coming from inside of my own head. The sound echoed through me until I too began to laugh, tears running in lines down my cheeks. I felt one of them slip down the slope of my nose and onto my lips, where I licked it away, tasting not the bitter salt of tears, but the rust of blood. The echoing laughter got lauder and louder until I fell into blackness.

When I awoke later, I ached to write, drawn to the word processor, my backup from the computer.

Maybe you think I'm a fool for believing in such a thing, that it would work, and even worse, that I'm insane to think that this apocalypse has been brought about by my actions. I believed in the core of my being in the art and the joy of writing, my ability to enjoy that gift was gone. My career a shambles and my personal life barely managed in the face of all the pressure I stood under, I had begun to unravel. The fact that I might ever consider doing such a thing should tell you this, but I swear to you that I know that this is true. That what I would write during all those long hours would be the tale you are living right this moment. Read further, my dear reader; don't doubt me by the mistakes I made in the beginning. Soon the truth will come to you.

    I couldn't explain the draw I felt toward my word processor, a gift from Robert that I'd barely used in these last few years of writing, perhaps some unseen force was again at work. I have no idea. As I sat before it and the screen booted up my fingers began to type words and before I knew what was happening there were seven chapters completed and another started. I smiled, relieved even in this moment of surreal possession, and as before my mind went blank and my vision hazed.

    What seemed like a few minutes later my hands stopped and I looked at the digital clock next to my keyboard. It was midnight! I had been typing a full sixteen hours! I could only look at the clock in disbelief, my mouth hanging loose and my eyes wide with shock. When I looked back to the word processor's screen, I fell from my chair in a dead faint. There on the screen were the words 'page 320 of 320'. I had never written more than sixteen pages at a time in my entire life as a writer.

When I awoke the next day, I picked myself up off the floor and started a shower. As I walked in I noticed my face in the mirror, there were brown streaks where the blood tears of yesterday had fallen. I looked for a moment, and choosing to ignore them, I stepped into the steaming water.

I stood there until the water ran cold and my skin wrinkled, no matter how I scrubbed, no matter how much soap I used, I couldn't get rid of the filth I felt deep inside of me. When I stepped out of the stall, shivering and sore, I looked into the fogged mirror. Even before I wiped away the remaining fog on the mirror, I saw the red and wrinkled flesh that wrapped my body. The blood trails were gone but my eyes had been puffed from weariness and my fingers were overstrained from working so long.

I called Robert after I'd dressed and tried to cover my puffy eyes with makeup.

"Hello, Robert." I said softly into the phone, my voice as weary as I felt. "Could you come over? I-I need to talk to you."

"Sure, love. I can be over in just a bit, but why?"

"I just need someone here, all right? I feel awful and you comfort me."

"I'll be there soon."

I hung up the phone and sat down to wait. It didn't take him long, we were only about ten minutes' drive apart. His knock was gentle and I'd already unlocked it once I'd gotten done with the phone. I didn't really care if anyone came after me in that moment.

"Come in, Robert."

When I looked up at him as he walked in the door, he stopped for a moment, looking me over and seeing all the exhaustion behind the make-up. He frowned with concern. "Just how late did you work last night? You look awful!"

"That does a lot for a girl's confidence, Robert." I said a little more snidely than I'd meant to.

"Oh, come off it, Abby! You mustn't work so late, you know, it worries me when I see you like this. As if the whole world's been gnawing at you."

"Yes." I replied quietly.

"Now why did you call me over so early? What did you need to tell me?"

"I wanted to talk to you about something, but it all seems silly now that I've thought about it."

"Are you sure?"

"Yes." I picked at a speck of something dark under my fingernails as I waited for him to go. When given a way out of some serious discussion Robert had always been quick to run.

His eyes went to the clock over the couch above me and, without taking his sight from it, he said. "Well then, Abby, let's not worry over it, all right?" Gathering himself out of the chair, he stood and got ready to go. "Damn, it's already getting too close; I've got to run to work." It was an hour yet before he had to go; I knew that by now, the clock agreed with my assessment. He ran to the door and left. As the door snicked softly shut behind him I picked up my coat and pocketbook, I had an urge to go out, maybe get some fresh air.

I rushed down the stairs and into the elevator. By the time I reached the door my momentum carried me straight through the door, nearly knocking over an elderly woman who glared at my impertinence. I went past her and on up the street, into the little bookstore on the corner. Bookstores were a place of solitude and quiet for me, the soothing sight and smell of them had a calming effect I had yet to find anywhere else. As I looked over their sparse and picked over collection I found myself remembering last year's writer's convention, where, to my boredom, I met many of the people on these shelves.

Many of them were narcissistic and full of themselves over work I had no interest in whatever. There was Jacob Midway, the short, bald, perverted little science fiction writer. Erin Staller, the writer of several high fantasy novel's about a Xena rip-off in leather and her nose in the air. Then there was Jared Eaglecrest, an attractive well-built and confident author of occult horror. Now that had been someone interesting! The drawback? He'd struck me as a little too into his work, a little too intense and virile in a sense that I found vaguely threatening no matter how attractive I found him.

I picked up his book and glanced it over, another occult horror in his usual vein but still interesting enough to consider as a purchase. I walked to the table and paid for it before heading back out onto the street. I bought a paper along with it; I'd been caught up these last few months and wanted to what was going on in the world.

As I look back on that day I realize that even before I

bought that book, all the way back to that conference at which I'd met him I'd made a terrible mistake in allowing him anywhere near me. Jared Teufel was a man perversely obsessed with the darker nature and aspects of the occult. This resulted in tremendously detailed novels about various spells and their results for power practitioners in hidden covens that held sway over entire populations that knew nothing about their existence.

That day was the first of many in which I would be witness to or hear of strange and horrifying experiences. It would not be long before I was overwhelmed.

In the present, I am plagued by the sound of the late Joey Warner creeping slowly over the roof of this car, seeking first safe purchase, and then a way to reach me in my cell. I find it hard to concentrate with him so near. As I write these words, I can hear his rotting hands tearing at the flimsy fabric of my sports car's roof and in a moment his already rotting hand will poke through. I thought that Joey was such a nice boy. It seems nothing can remain in death. Back to the past then, and away from this horror.

As I walked toward the neighboring street on my path

toward home I heard tires skidding and a terrible gurgling scream that I recognize as a man's. Before I even reached the scene I knew that the voice was Robert's and a horrid knowledge came to me, that he was dead or dying, beyond any feeling I had for him. My heart pounded with fear and regret as my eyes fell on the him and I wondered how much of this was my fault, if I had brought it about with my terrible deeds and senseless need for recognition.

I can only stare in numb horror, my mouth quivering with disgust and incomprehension. Robert had been torn in half somehow, his torso wrapped in the grate of a semi and his legs left on the ground. Tendons, muscle, veins, and arteries hung between the halves that had for so long made him up, the internal organs of his body slipping from the gap as he writhed in pain. A terrible sound of agony came from him and I knew that he was already beyond my reach, not dead but dying, gone mad and irretrievable with the horrific sensation moving through him. I try not to look at his face, afraid to see what expression I might find there. Robert had been my lover for the last five years, though we had never been in love I thought that some emotion should rise in me, some remorse for past mistakes or words, but there was only revulsion and a dull numbness.

I still fail to understand what happened next. I started to laugh in the midst of that terrible scene, with so many people looking in gap-mouthed horror at what had befallen my lover. It was long and braying, a terrible lunatic laughter that earned me disgusted stares and disbelief. I couldn't make it stop as I moved away, the crowd breaking and stepping back from me as if my madness were catching.

Damn! I've run out of gas! The idea of even getting out of this car, let alone walking to find gas, strikes me as idiotic. In my haste I had forgotten to get fuel, though I doubt I'd have had the time to get it in any case. I'm lucky that this had been the landscaper's car, some of Charlie's equipment could be useful. Too bad then that Charlie is gone, he was a good man. Now, my reader, I bid you farewell. If these are my last words you might wonder what became of me or what it was that caused all of this. For now, to me, it means nothing. I only hope to live.

--The End--